Voyage to a Free Land

1630

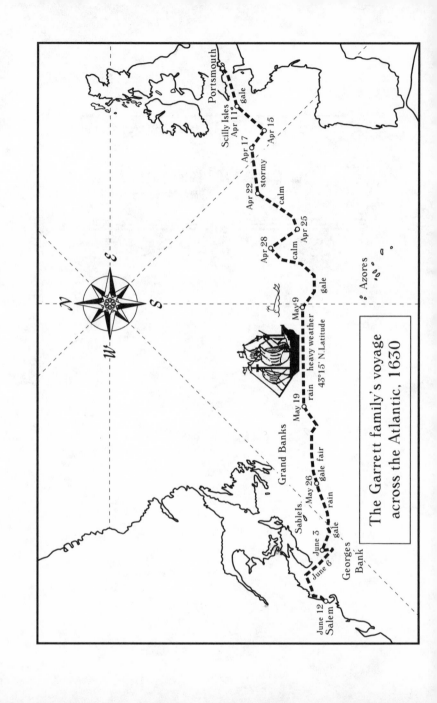

The Garrett family's voyage across the Atlantic, 1630

Portsmouth
Scilly Isles
Apr 11
gale
Apr 17
stormy
Apr 22
calm
Apr 25
Apr 28
calm
gale
May 9
heavy weather
43°15' N. Latitude
May 19
rain
Grand Banks
May 26
gale fair
rain
June 3
gale
Sable Is.
Georges Bank
June 6
June 12
Salem
Azores
Apr 15

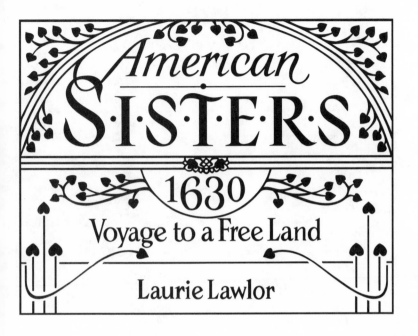

American SISTERS

1630
Voyage to a Free Land

Laurie Lawlor

A MINSTREL® HARDCOVER
PUBLISHED BY POCKET BOOKS

New York   London   Toronto   Sydney   Tokyo   Singapore

A MINSTREL HARDCOVER

A Minstrel Book published by
POCKET BOOKS, a division of Simon & Schuster Inc.
1230 Avenue of the Americas, New York, NY 10020

ISBN: 0-671-01552-4

First Minstrel Books hardcover printing January 1999

10 9 8 7 6 5 4 3 2 1

A MINSTREL BOOK and colophon are registered trademarks of
Simon & Schuster Inc.

Cover illustration by Franco Accornero

Printed in the U.S.A.

RRDHB / ✹

For Phyllis Trautman O'Neill
also fondly known as Aunt Sis

Books by Laurie Lawlor

The Worm Club
How to Survive the Third Grade
Addie Across the Prairie
Addie's Long Summer
Addie's Dakota Winter
George on His Own
Gold in the Hills
Little Women *(a movie novelization)*

Heartland series
Heartland: Come Away with Me
Heartland: Take to the Sky
Heartland: Luck Follows Me

American Sisters series
West Along the Wagon Road 1852
A *Titanic* Journey Across the Sea 1912
Voyage to a Free Land 1630

Voyage to a Free Land

1630

"Come away from the gate, Hannah," Abigail called to her sister from where she was seated beneath the budding apple tree in Grandmother Garrett's garden.

"Someone needs help. Shouldn't we answer?" replied Hannah, who was ten years old. She tiptoed and yet still wasn't tall enough to see over the thick brambly hedge that ran around the garden on all four sides. The hedgerow's bare branches scraped in the raw wind. From a nearby field wafted the rich smell of just-plowed earth.

"We can get no work," a pitiful voice cried

from the other side of the hedge. "Nor have we no money. And if we should steal, we should be hanged."

Abigail frowned. Unlike Hannah, who had a round face, dimples, and merry dark eyes, Abigail's eyes were gray blue, the color of February ice. Abigail's face was as plain as a pike staff, except when she smiled, which wasn't often.

Daintily, Abigail took another nibble of the warm, fragrant chunk of gingerbread she held in her lap. "So many beggars I never saw!" she exclaimed. "It's probably another one of the lazy, idle people who've brought horrible, not-to-be-named sins to Chelmsford. 'Perpetual drunkenness, frays, and bloodshed,' Father says. Beggars spend all their time filching and stealing."

Hannah bit her lip. "What should I do? What should I say?"

"Nothing. Don't answer. I forbid you."

Abigail was twelve years old. So she must know everything, didn't she? Desperately Hannah glanced at the spotless leaded pane on the first floor of Grandmother's house. Inside Father and Goody Garrett, their stepmother, were saying last goodbyes to Grandmother and Caleb, Hannah and Abigail's eldest brother. What if Father and the others were watching her out the window?

"We're starving," the voice wailed, louder this time. "Your worshipfulness, give us something to eat."

Hannah's brow furrowed. She examined her own piece of half-eaten gingerbread. That very day they were leaving for London. Father said their voyage across the wide sea to America might take months. When would she ever taste Grandmother's special delicacy again?

A dirty hand no bigger than a child's—scabbed and half-gloved against the cold—gripped the top of the wooden gate. The iron latch rattled. "Don't send us away empty-handed."

Hannah looked over her shoulder at her sister, who had finished eating her treat and was now busy braiding long strands of dried grass. "Take this," Hannah hissed and quickly thrust the gingerbread over the gate. "Thou art welcome for all of it." The sweet brown cake vanished. Through a crack between the slats she caught a glimpse of a small hooded figure limping quickly away.

"What did you just do?" Abigail demanded and jumped to her feet. "What did you just say?"

"Nothing."

Abigail joined her sister and peered suspiciously over the top of the gate. "Lying is a sin. You know what Father will do when he finds out you disobeyed me and then told a falsehood."

Miserably Hannah nodded. She rubbed her sticky hands against the folds of her cloak. "I gave her my gingerbread."

"The beggar was a woman?"

Hannah shrugged. "I couldn't see her very well. Maybe she was a young girl."

Abigail put a finger to her thin lips. Her eyes looked frightened. "Did she mumble a curse?"

"I don't think so. She didn't say anything. She just took the gingerbread and hurried out of sight."

"A witch," Abigail said in a low voice. "You've heard what's been happening around Essex. Witches disguised as beggars making demands. If they're refused, cows don't calve. Geese desert their nests. Mares die. Beasts drown in ditches."

Hannah was about to bite her fingernails when she noticed her sister's scowl and thought better of the idea. Instead, she tucked a strand of brown hair inside her linen coif, the small close-fitting cap Grandmother had edged with lace. "Perhaps," Hannah said slowly, carefully, "it's a good thing I gave the beggar what she wanted."

"It would be a terrible tragedy," Abigail replied in a grudging voice, "to have a witch's curse upon us before we sail."

"Then you won't tell Father?"

"Not this time. Of course, God knows. God knows everything. He sees everything. He's the only one who can send your soul to burn in eternal damnation."

Miserably Hannah nodded. She felt worse than ever. *Is there nowhere in all the world to hide?*

Abigail smiled down at her sister. Her expression was sweet and superior. "New England is an earthly paradise," she said. "There are no beggars. No witches. Everything is perfect. Just wait, you'll see." She linked arms with Hannah and marched her around the garden, following the worn flagstone path. They stepped from stone to stone at exactly the same moment, almost as if they were the same person. As they walked, they chanted:

> *"One, two, three, four,*
> *Mary at the kitchen door.*
> *Five, six, seven, eight.*
> *Mary at the garden gate."*

Abigail came to a sudden halt. "Tell dreams," she announced.

"Whose turn?"

"Put out your fists."

Hannah held out her hands, palms down, fingers curled shut. Abigail touched each of her sister's fists, then her own as she called out:

> *"Ikkamy, dukkamy, alligar, mole*
> *Dick slew alligar slum,*
> *Hukka pukka, Peter's gum*
> *Francis."*

Her hand rested on Hannah's fist. Hannah cleared her throat. "It's about our journey, I think. You were in the dream, too."

Abigail nodded approvingly.

"I dreamed we sailed to a land very far away where we found a wonderful house in the air, very fine and shiny like the inside of oyster shells. A great man as big as a house came out with a great fire in his head." Hannah motioned with swoops of her arms. "He came to the ground. The house vanished inside a snail. And you and I crept around on the ground like frogs."

Abigail did not look pleased. "Like frogs?"

"Frogs are happy, winsome creatures," Hannah insisted. She reached inside her pocket, a flat linen bag she wore tied around her waist with two long ribbons. Carefully she uncurled each finger just enough so that Abigail could see what she'd found. "See how merrily my frog grins?"

Abigail shrieked. "Hideous! Loathsome! Don't think for a moment that you're going to bring that monster with us all the way to London."

Hannah laughed. She crouched near the

hedgerow and gently placed the tiny frog on the ground. The frog made a few halfhearted jumps before escaping from the garden. "Goodbye, dear frog," she whispered. "Remember me."

"Daughters of mine!" Father called from Grandmother's doorway. "Come inside and say goodbye. Your grandmother and brother are waiting." Hannah stood up and brushed her hands together. She followed her sister into the frame-and-siding house with the steep thatched roof.

As the girls entered Grandmother's hall, Abigail turned to Hannah and hissed, "Remember, sing not. Hum not. Wiggle not."

Hannah sighed.

The hall was dark and smelled of the smoke of smoldering peat burning in the open fireplace of brick and stone. The raftered ceiling danced with shadows. In the middle of the room stood a long wooden table and four stools. Grandmother sat in her usual place beside the fire in the only chair with a cushion. She gripped her walking stick. Goody Garrett, their stepmother, industriously knitted while seated on a hard, backless bench. Nearby, Caleb leaned against the wall. He winked at Hannah.

"Hannah and Abigail," Father said, "please give your grandmother the respect due her."

Abigail curtsied. Hannah curtsied. Abigail gave her sister a slight shove. Hannah slipped the hood back from her head and took a few steps toward Grandmother. In the firelight she could see the gaps where Grandmother's teeth had once been. A hair sprouted from her chin. She leaned forward and extended her cheek in Hannah's direction. Obediently Hannah kissed her soft, wrinkled skin. Abigail did the same. Both girls quickly withdrew from striking range of Grandmother's handy walking stick.

"So you're off to a hideous, desolate wilderness full of wild beasts and wild men," Grandmother said. Her eyes were rheumy and cloudy, but she stared intently at Hannah. Abigail prodded her to speak.

Hannah gulped. "Yes, Grandmother."

"We are building a new Zion in America," Father said. Hannah took a few steps backward.

She held Father's big, calloused hand and hid behind him as best she could.

"Why must you go so early in spring? Why not wait for warmer weather?" Grandmother demanded. "You are certain to meet with snow-storms — not to mention man-eating fish and terrible pirates."

Father sighed. "I have explained this all before, Mother. Winthrop's ships sail from London as soon as he's ready. The voyage may be ten, twelve weeks or more. We must arrive in New England early to begin planting. There is much work to be done. I must set up my shoemaking business and build a house."

"I don't understand your hurry," Grandmother insisted. "Why not wait till next year?"

"There's not a moment to lose now that there's talk that Parliament will soon be dissolved," Father insisted. "Who knows what will happen to us then? Pastor Hooker predicts some heavy affliction upon this land. I'm afraid the Lord's patience may run out soon. New England will provide a shelter and a hiding place for the righteous."

Grandmother spat into the fire. "What does Hooker know? I've heard him speak to those mobs in Chelmsford. Full of fire and thunder. He handles his mighty spirit as if it were a mad mastiff on a chain. How can you follow a man like that?"

"He's a learned preacher," Goody Garrett said in a shrill voice. "He has a great gift. He speaks the truth. Mother Garrett, you should take heed of wronging a praying minister."

Hannah and Abigail exchanged looks of astonishment. No one ever openly corrected Grandmother—not even Father.

"Bah!" Grandmother said. She thumped her walking stick on the floor. She swiveled and fixed her awful stare on Father. "You are running away. You are abandoning your country. You are abandoning your first wife, bless her soul, and the five little babes laid to rest in the cemetery. *And* you are abandoning me."

Father let go of Hannah's hand. "Now, now, Mother." He lifted his palms as if he could stop Grandmother's stinging words from flying through the air. "No one is abandoning you. Caleb will be here. He will take care of you."

Caleb unfolded his long legs. He was nearly twenty-one, just a year younger than Goody Garrett. "I am not abandoning you, Grandmother," he said, and smiled his most charming smile. "How could I leave? The glovers' trade is better than ever, no matter who runs the country. Isn't that right, Dumpling?" He turned to Hannah, using the pet name he'd given her as a toddler when she was as plump as a Norfolk dumpling.

Hannah tried to smile. But she did not want to leave Caleb behind. He was always quick with a ready joke. He did not correct her as Abigail did. He did not frown at her the way their stepmother did. Unlike Father, who was always too busy, Caleb took her ice-skating on the shallow pond. He carried her on his back when she was too tired to walk all the way home. What would she do without him?

"Help me pack the last box in the cart, will you, Hannah?" Caleb asked.

Glad to escape Grandmother's dark, smoky hall, Hannah followed her brother outside. The two-wheeled cart was already piled high with all the belongings they would take with them on the ship.

"Don't look so full of woe, Hannah. A sorrowful face does not become you," Caleb said. "You will write to me, won't you?" He glanced toward the doorway. "And when I sell my business and the time is right," he added in a low, confidential voice, "I will come across the ocean, too."

"You will?" Hannah asked. "When? When will you come to America?"

"Soon enough."

"In a month? A year? Tell me."

Caleb smiled and sang in his sweetest voice:

> *"When daffodils begin to peer,*
> *With hey! The doxy o'er the dale,*
> *Why, then comes in the sweet o' the year;*
> *For the red blood reigns in winter's pale."*

Somehow Caleb's song did not cheer Hannah. Tears suddenly clouded her eyes. "What if I never see you again?"

Caleb rested his hand gently on her head. "Then we will meet in heaven."

Hannah sniffed loudly. She was not altogether certain she'd ever make it to heaven—at least, that was what Abigail reminded her almost daily. "Will you write to me?"

"Most certainly," Caleb promised. "And I shall send you news from your friends, the frogs, and all creatures everywhere in Essex who are full of delights."

Hannah smiled.

"Singing birds. Sporting fish. Even the very insects you so love. All a marvelous display of infinite goodness," Caleb said and winked. He took something from his pocket. It was a long, narrow black rock pointed at one end like the beak of a bird. "And here is something for you to take along to remember me."

Hannah turned the six-inch rock over and over in her hands. "What is it?"

"A thunderbolt. I picked it up near the heath lands of Suffolk after a particularly powerful tempest. Plenty of lightning flashing and thunder. This thunderbolt was lying in a field and felt right warm, having just fallen from the sky. Keep it for luck."

Hannah tucked the lucky thunderbolt inside her pocket and gave her dear brother one last hug.

My Record of Remarkables

February 21, 1630

I, Abigail Garrett, vow to write here in this small secret book every day I am able. This will be a pious exercise to record and remind myself of God's goodness in saving me from losses and grief and in leading me to salvation through suffering. I should praise my Dear Father for providing me and my sister with an excellent education so that we may read the Bible and scriptures. His understanding and generosity allow me to write here.

Our beloved Reverend Hooker exhorted those of us leaving for America to keep a list of our resolutions and record God's providences in our daily life. THESE ARE FOR MY EYES AND GOD'S ALONE. If my sister should find this book AND READ THIS FAR I warn her to STOP now and put this away and not look at it again or suffer God's AWFUL WRATH. . . .

Myself I seek to know. We leave soon for the New World, and I may never again see England or the face of my dear Kitty, who has been sent out to learn house-wifery in Dedham. Her Fate might have been mine, too, if it weren't that my Dear Father decided to make this Great Sacrifice and go across the Ocean to begin a New Life. Reverend Hooker says we should view our-selves as Pilgrims on a Journey to God and Heaven. "We are all in a great spiritual battle between Good and Evil, God and Satan," he says.

I confess I am troubled. It is a very long Dangerous way to America. I think of my Tender Mother often, and it makes me very sad. How will I ever measure up to her Great Heart? I try to protect my only sister as best I can, just as my Mother would. Hannah is of a wonderful sweetness, calmness, and universal benevolence of Mind. She will sometimes go About from Place to Place singing sweetly and Seems to be always full of Joy and Pleasure and no one knows for what. *She loves to be alone, walking in the fields and groves and seems to have someone Invisible always conversing with her.*

She is so unaware of the Wickedness of the World. How will I keep my Eye on her safety every Moment? My worst fear is that she should be taken from me and be gone forever like Tender Mother who is surely in Heaven.

I write here not to please the Fancy but to tell the Truth. Today at Grandmother's we said our Farewells, and I could not help but notice an Unholy Glance between my brother Caleb and my new Stepmother. I promised my Grandmother not to laugh, play, run fast, or sleep during sermons on Sabbath. She even forbade that I eat my favorite sucket—dried sweet meats and candied orange peel. I think it will be very hard to keep this promise.

I must keep a better watch over my heart and keep my thoughts close to good things and not Suffer a Vain or Worldly thought lest it draw the Heart to delight in It. I resolve never to lose one moment of time but to improve it in the most profitable way I possibly can.

Chapter

2

To my deare and very loving brother
Mr. Caleb Garrett at Chelmsford:

Deare Brother, — My humble dutie remembered to you. We arrived in good speed in
spite of miry roads. London brims with so
many people, I am dizzy. The Thames
smells strong enough to stop a church clock.
Boatmen call out "Eastward-ho" and
"Westward-ho" and will take you where you
want to go. We saw a gilded barge with roy-
alty and also criminals chained to the banks
of the river. On Temple Bar are fresh-severed
heads on pikes that I could not look at, but
Abigail did and she said the eyes were pecked

out. So many houses! So many people! The
streets and alleyways are narrow, cobbled,
and slimy with garbage and slops. Goody
Garrett vomited dreadfully. Kites are graceful
birds that make their nests with rags and anything they can find in the forks of trees. They
eat the garbage along the river. Did I tell you
how deafening it is here? So many loud
noises—singing on the street and traders
yelling and coach-wheels on the cobbles and
swordfights. Father says he is glad we are
leaving, for this is a city of terrible sin. Our
ship sails tomorrow down the Thames into
the English Channel to the straits of Dover
and on to the Isle of Wight. I will write you
again once we reach Southampton.

Commend my blessing to Grandmother.
Time will suffer me to write no more; fare
you well always in the Lord, in Whom I rest.

> Your humble sister,
> Hannah
> at Red Wolf Inn, London
> February 23, 1630

❧

The London dock was crowded with people and cargo all bound for exotic locations. Tall ships stood cheek by jowl, their enormous masts moving and swaying as the wind slipped through the forest of wood and rope. Hannah held Abigail's hand tightly and followed her father as he stepped over coiled rope and boxes and bags and bales. Some had strange foreign writing Hannah could not read. Everywhere was chaos and confusion. Men rushed about loading and unloading, shouting and calling to one another in colorful oaths that Goody Garrett found so distressing, she covered her ears.

Father led the horse and cart along the road. "Can thou tell me where I might find the *Arbella?*" he called out to a man who sauntered past. The man wore a short blue jacket, a red waistcoat, and a checked shirt with a scarf tied loosely around his neck.

The man tipped his hat. "What master, your worship?"

"I believe his name is Captain Peter Milborne. The ship's headed for Massachusetts Bay."

The man scratched his head, which was amply covered with thick black matted hair. "You one of the cursed Saints?"

Father stood up straight. "If you mean are we the Children of God, yes. It is our pleasure to cross the ocean and seek a new life."

The man laughed rudely. "He that would go to sea for pleasure, would go to hell for pastime! Try the next dock."

Father's face flushed with anger. "Thou art a saucy fellow, Sailor!" He turned abruptly on his heel and kept walking, guiding Goody Garrett as he went. Abigail and Hannah had to lift their long skirts and practically run to keep up with him.

"What did he say, Father?" Abigail demanded. Hannah chimed up, "He said—"

"Never mind," Father interrupted. "Keep walking."

Eventually they found a ship with a great eagle projecting from her bow. The word *Arbella* was painted in gleaming letters on the ship's massive wooden hull. "Look at that!" Hannah said in a low voice. She had never seen anything so impressive. How did a creation so large and heavy and solid-looking stay afloat? There was no door visible anywhere. How would they manage to climb inside? Suddenly a small figure scaled the side of the ship as swiftly as a spider up a wall. He seemed to be clinging to a rope.

"I hope they don't expect us to climb that, too," Goody Garrett said. She leaned wearily against the cart of goods.

"The ship's 350 tons. She has fifty-two seamen on board," Father said proudly. "And twenty-eight guns. The *Arbella* is the largest of the Massachusetts Bay Company fleet. She's the flagship."

"Why, Father, is the ship a 'she'?" Hannah asked. She craned her neck for another glimpse of the spiderlike man. Where had he gone? "And why do we need guns on the ship? Will they be used to shoot man-eating fish?"

"What stupid questions!" Abigail muttered.

"I cannot tell you everything you wish to know just now," Father said distractedly. "We must get our goods on board before one of these disreputable people tries to steal something. Daughters of mine, go and amuse yourselves nearby. But do not wander far. We are to sail at the next tide."

Hannah wanted to ask her sister what a tide was but decided Abigail might make fun of her again, and so she kept her mouth shut.

Abigail took Hannah by the hand. Hannah felt unwilling to leave the ship after it had taken them so long to find it. A group of sailors carrying bags over their shoulders wandered past. "Where should we go?" Hannah asked. "What should we do?"

"If we walk along the wharf we won't get lost," Abigail said.

Hannah sniffed the air. It smelled of fish and pitch and hemp. Was that how the ocean would smell, too? Nearby a woman in a ragged dress was selling hot chestnuts. The delicious roasting aroma made Hannah's stomach growl.

"Will you buy any tape?" called a gaudily dressed peddler with one eye. He was loaded down with ribbons and spools. "Or lace for your cape, my dainty duck, my dear-a? Any silk, any thread, any toys for your head?"

Abigail stared longingly at a woman who strutted past in a bright yellow hat with a large brim and jeweled headband adorned with a long white plume. Around her neck she wore an impressive oval ruff. "I might get into one of my frolics. Just look at that hat!" Abigail said and sighed. "May God forgive my vanity."

"But what is wrong with her face?" Hannah whispered. She stared at the dazzling woman with bright red dots. Black stars and half moons adorned her cheeks, chin, and forehead. "Do you suppose she has the plague?"

Abigail shrugged. The two girls kept walking and soon came upon a man carrying a strange-looking child with the face of a whiskered old man. The child was small and thin, as if he had not eaten in a very long time. Around his neck he wore a scarf and the same breeches as the saucy sailor they had met earlier. Instead of carrying the baby in a normal fashion, the father lifted the scrawny child upon his shoulder.

Hannah let go of her sister's hand. "Look at his wee fingers and ears!" Hannah exclaimed and pointed. But Abigail had spotted the yellowhatted plague woman again and kept following her from a safe distance.

The strange baby threw a peanut. It hit Hannah squarely on the forehead. "Ouch!" she cried. "Sir, thine child is a rude one!"

The man laughed. "'Tis a monkey, miss. My own son don't look as bad as him." He placed the monkey on the ground, and the man began singing in a loud, off-key voice.

"You talk of New England; I truly believe
   Old England's grown new and doth us deceive.
   I'll ask you a question or two, by your leave;
      And is not old England grown new?

"New fashions in houses, new fashions at table,
   The old servants discharged, the new are more able;
   And every old custom is but an old fable!
      And is not old England grown new?"

As the man sang, the little furry fellow danced and frolicked in such a human way that Hannah thought he might at any moment begin singing, too. She clapped and the monkey tumbled and screeched. He took off his small blue cap and politely held it out for Hannah and the growing crowd around her.

"He's asking for a coin or two," the man announced.

Money jingled on the cobblestones. The monkey stood in front of Hannah and cocked its head to one side and looked at her with piercing black, humanlike eyes that made Hannah suddenly feel uneasy. "I . . . I haven't any money," she stammered.

The man grunted and lifted the monkey to his shoulder and swiftly walked away. Another crowd of travelers rushed past. Hannah looked all around but could not see her sister anywhere.

"Abigail!" Hannah called. On every side were unfamiliar faces. She hurried along the winding street, searching for a glimpse of her sister's black cloak. There! She recognized Abigail's back and the peak of her hood. She ran, breathless, and reached out.

"Who art thou? Leave go my sleeve!" the angry, pock-faced young woman exclaimed and shook herself free.

"Beg pardon," Hannah said. Sweat streamed down her forehead as she raced along the street, ducking here and there, for a better glimpse of the people ahead or behind her. Wagons and carts rolled past. Where was the wharf? What if she missed the tide—whatever that might be? Hannah stumbled, exhausted. She looked up and saw kites reeling overhead. She'd follow them. But the longer she tracked the kites, the more confused and lost she felt. Nothing looked familiar. The kites flapped out of sight.

"Are you lost, miss?" a fiery-faced man called from a doorway. He wore the same outfit as the saucy fellow who had insulted Father earlier that day. He was a short, stout man with red hair. A pipe protruded from one corner of his smiling mouth. His mocking expression convinced Hannah not to talk to him. What if he insulted her the way that other sailor had insulted Father?

She ran down an alley and leaned against a wall to catch her breath. Overhead someone opened a window. Dirty water, stale beer, apple peels, eggshells, and rotten potato splashed down into the cobblestone streets. Hannah wiped the mess from her arm and began to cry.

She was lost forever. The tide would come and her family would leave without her. She'd never find Abigail or Father or Goody Garrett again. She'd be abandoned for the rest of her life in this horrible city. She sobbed louder. But no one stopped to help her. Carts and crowds scurried past. No one asked her what she was doing all by herself.

Hannah reached inside her pocket to find her handkerchief. She found instead Caleb's thunderbolt. The stone felt cool and comforting against her hot, wet cheek. She closed her eyes. She tried to imagine where her sister might be. Why had she gone off and left her? Perhaps she was lost, too.

Suddenly Hannah heard the sound of a familiar voice. "Hannah!"

"Abigail!" Hannah cried, overjoyed to see her sister. She quickly replaced the thunderbolt in her pocket. Perhaps Caleb was right. Perhaps the thunderbolt really could bring her good fortune.

"I've looked and looked for you!" Abigail exclaimed as she embraced her sister. Then she held her sister's shoulders and looked directly into Hannah's dark eyes. "You are never to go out, unless I am with you. Do you understand?"

Hannah nodded. All the way back to the *Arbella*, she did not once let go of Abigail's hand. How could she ever have imagined Abigail as anything less than the very best sister in all the world?

My Record of Remarkables

February 24, 1630

I must maintain a strict and Constant Watch over myself against all Temptations, that I do not forsake and forget God, and particularly I do not grow slack in Secret Religion. I must strive to retire often from the vain world, from all its bubbles and empty shadows and vain amusements and converse with God Alone and seek Divine grace and Comfort, the least Drop of which is worth more than all the riches, gaiety, pleasures, and entertainments of the whole world. . . .

Even here in this sinful City there are Providences. I was so enthralled by my own vanity, Following a Beautiful Hat, that I lost my sister in a terrible crowd. And I cried out, "Oh, My Lord, help me if you Will!" And I looked and looked for her, fearful she should be run over by a Wild Horse or Kidnapped or Murdered. But Angels were Watching and Led me to her, and I thank God again and again for giving me another chance to prove I am Worthy and to try not to be Snared by Bright Hats, which are my Great weakness.

In thankfulness as I walked through the crowded Streets with my Newly found Sister, I secretly Blessed thousands of strangers who never knew I did it. I offered them Secret Wishes after this manner sent unto Heaven for them. For example, if I saw a Tall Man I said to myself, "Lord, give this man high Attainments in Christianity." If I saw a Lame man, I said, "Lord, help this man Walk upright."

When we again rejoined my great-bellied step-mother, I decided not to tell her of Hannah's wandering for fear that she would punish my sister. Once in one of her Vile Moods she threatened to send Hannah far away from me. I know a cruel master in Berk-

shire who would have her, says she. And when I said I would tell Dear Father, she says to me she'll send Hannah even farther—all the way to North Umberland.

God spare me and my sister from her Ill Tempers.

Chapter

3

Dear Brother and Kind Friend Caleb
at Chelmsford:

I pray that you are well and receive this
letter before we sail. At last we have arrived
in Southampton, where we await more passengers and the *Jewel*, the *Ambrose*, and the
Talbot, the three other ships that will travel
with us. We are glad to leave London. Did I
tell you how difficult it is to step into a small
boat in the Thames when a swell is rising?
My knees doubled up and I fell to the bottom of the boat, which gave everyone a
good laugh—especially Abigail, who consid-

ers herself an expert sailor even though she can swim no better than I.

We cruised the English Channel in the *Arbella* and arrived at the Isle of Wight and the great port of Southampton. At last I could see the wide, wide ocean, which looks as flat as the biggest, open meadows in Essex. But what a remarkable loud roar the ocean makes! Father called me a whimsical child for wanting to taste it with my finger. I had heard the ocean is not filthy like the Thames but very salty, which is true. I stared very hard, but I could not see America. I believe this voyage will take much longer than I thought.

We are now disembarked at Portsmouth and staying temporarily at the Blackwatch Inn in one room. Father is distressed that all our frantic hurry has been useless. He complains that each day of delay costs him sixpence to pay for our lodging. I hope that our victuals will not be half-eaten up before we go from the coast of England. We are trapped here while tons of goods are loaded on board the ship. The captain is waiting for signed papers of some sort from officials and searchers, I have overheard. Some of the Saints traveling with us can be seen strolling the docks. Some consult dockside fortune-tellers, and I wonder what they tell them. Some visit taverns. Father prays. Goody Garrett prays. Father says delay is a trial to test our faith. Abigail and I go exploring. She has been very kind to me and even shared her syllabub from the Blackwatch. We drank the sweet-flavored milk drink through straws just like grown-up ladies.

Though you are at so great a distance from us, God is everywhere. Abigail tells me to write that we are all, through the Divine goodness, in a tolerable state of health with the exception of our stepmother, who has some stomach pains.

Your very affectionate sister,
Hannah in Southampton
March 10, 1630

At daybreak on a blustery morning on March 20, Hannah awoke to the sound of gulls. Her sister shook her shoulder. "Today! Father says we sail today. Make ready."

Excitedly Hannah and her family gathered up their few belongings. Goody Garrett was so flustered, she tied her coif on her head inside out and had to be reminded by Father how unseemly she looked. He paid the innkeeper. The family hurried to the dock without pausing to eat even a crust of bread.

The *Arbella* was anchored in the middle of the harbor. A sharp report of a cannon and white smoke suddenly billowed from the hull of the ship. "What does that mean?" Hannah asked Father. "Is there to be a battle?"

"No, daughter of mine. The cannon means we must get aboard as soon as we are able or we will be left behind," Father said with a worried expression. "Our goods are loaded. Now we must find a boatman to take us to the ship." He waved his arm, and a strong rower with a long, fragile boat pulled up beside the dock.

"Where to, sir?" the boatman called.

"The *Arbella*." Father helped Goody Garrett into the boat. Hannah gripped Father's hand tightly so that this time she did not tumble. The boat lurched. Abigail's face turned as pale as sea foam.

Hannah smiled at her. "You are an expert sailor," she said.

Abigail only grimaced.

The boatman began to row with all his might. The small boat was bucked by large, gray waves. Hannah pulled her cloak around her to keep away the salt spray. The clean sharp sea smell was mixed with the smell of tar and paint and cordage from the dockyard. *Boom!* There was another sharp report of cannon from the *Arbella*. Another cannon answered from shore.

"Can thou row faster?" Father shouted over the sound of the splashing waves. "I see the flag raised aboard ship."

The oarsman barked an oath. "I'm going as fast as I'm going," he snarled.

Little by little, Hannah could make out the flag's scarlet cross of Saint George showing bravely on the field of white. The *Arbella* rolled with heavy skittishness. The ship towered over them like an enormous, slippery wooden wall, rising and falling in the dangerous cold water. The little boat danced and dipped alongside as if it would be crushed or sucked under at any moment. *How will we ever get on board?* Hannah glanced at her sister. Abigail's face had turned the color of moldy cheese.

A sailor above them on the *Arbella* lowered the gangway, a long wooden plank. "Hop aboard!" the grinning boatman prompted Father.

Father crawled to the entering port. He held out his hand and helped Hannah, Abigail, and Goody Garrett aboard.

As Hannah was hoisted on to the rocking deck, she became aware of how much more crowded the ship had suddenly become since they left London. A hundred new passengers hovered about, looking over the sides toward land. She did not recognize any familiar faces from Chelmsford. Who were these people? Where had they come from? There were men and women, boys and girls of all shapes and sizes. Some ran and shouted along the deck. Others huddled out of the wind, nearly as green as Abigail. Shots were fired from somewhere on ship. Trumpets blared. Flags waved. And the crowd on deck shouted and waved their hats to the faraway crowd on the Portsmouth dock.

"Goodbye!" Hannah cried, caught up in the great enthusiasm of the moment. She was so busy cheering, she did not notice that her sister had disappeared.

Rough-looking sailors formed a circle around a wheel-like contraption and began pushing with all their might in a circle. Hannah watched the iron anchor being hauled up dripping on its tarred cable.

"Two men above to the foretop to cut the ribbons and let the foresail fall!" someone shouted.

What language is this? Hannah wondered. She watched wide-eyed as another group of sailors began pulling on ropes and lifting a gigantic flapping gray canvas sail. As they pulled, they sang.

"Tell 'em all, tell 'em all,
 Gallowbirds all, gallowbirds all,
 Great and small, great and small,
 One and all, one and all."

Now came more shouts and orders. "Make fast the halyards—set your topsails—haul your topsail sheets—veer your lifters and your topsail braces—hoist the topsail higher—haul taut the topsail bowline—hoist the mizzen and change it over to leeward—sway the sheets and the belaying pins—haul the braces to the yard."

Hannah watched two men at one end of the ship holding tight to a smaller wooden wheel held upright. "Mate, keep her full and by, a-luff. . . . Come no higher. . . . Hold your tiller steady as you are."

Wind suddenly filled the sails. When Hannah looked straight up, she could barely see the top of the tallest wooden pole that stood in the center of the ship—taller than the biggest tree in Chelmsford. Two more wooden poles with sails, slightly smaller, stood at each end. Near the eagle figurehead unfurled another small sail. Wind hummed through countless ropes extended every which way. Canvas flapped and slammed. Wood creaked. Waves thudded and crashed against the boat. Sailors rushed about, shouting incomprehensible orders. The language, the customs — everything seemed so strange. *What world am I in? Is this a dream?* Desperately she looked about for Abigail. She wanted the comfort of a familiar face.

The wooden deck below her feet suddenly shifted and lurched. She tripped over a coil of rope and lurched headfirst into a skinny, rabbit-faced boy.

"Beg pardon," she said nervously and righted herself. "Lost my balance." She glared down at the rope as if her stumbling was all its fault.

"This ship's got enough skeins, coils, and tangles to remind a person of the gallows," the boy said darkly. "I suppose *that* is a comfort if you prefer hanging to drowning."

Hannah looked curiously at the raggedy boy with curly brown hair and serious gray eyes. She found his familiarity annoying. She would remind him of his place. "Does *thou* have a name? Who art *thou?*"

"I am my own self."

Hannah rolled her eyes. "Does thou have a mother?"

"No."

"A father?"

"No."

"A master?"

"Yes. But he is more of an old mule than a man. See how he brays?" The boy pointed to an ancient bearded man across the way who shrieked and stomped in anger at another servant. "He's a mad jack in his mood."

Hannah giggled. "Thou art saucy."

"I am," the boy said and smiled proudly. "My name is Zachariah Punt. But you may call me Zach. Or Saucy Zach if you wish."

"My name is Hannah Garrett and I just lost my family."

Zach made a sad face. "Did they drown? Or die of the pox?"

"Neither!" Hannah said and laughed. She had never met anyone quite like Zachariah Punt.

"They wandered off and left me, and now I don't know where they are."

"Well, I will be happy to help you find them. I know my way everywhere about this ship. Follow me." He dodged a group of angry younger children chasing a larger boy. "Do you see up there?"

Hannah nodded. She peered up to the tallest level of the ship, reached by a set of stairs. She had glimpsed a wheel up there and much shouting earlier.

"That is the quarterdeck. Captain Milborne's cabin is up there and an untethered goat and fowls in coops. I don't think your family is up there. Most passengers are not allowed."

"Who's that then?" Hannah asked, pointing. A woman in a bright cape and hood and mask appeared on the deck with two other women and several young ladies, all dressed in long black embroidered velvet jackets fastened by bows of purple ribbon. Their full dark skirts were embroidered as well, and around their necks were lace ruffs. Each carried sable muffs. They turned and looked down on the deck. The youngest, who appeared to be only a few years older than Abigail, gave Hannah a haughty glance.

Zach took off his large-brimmed hat and made a sweeping bow. Hannah curtsied.

"Those are what you call your gentle folks or your better sort," Zach said in a low voice. "Lady Arbella Johnson and the rest. They have their own great cabin on the quarterdeck. That's where they dine on quail and sweetmeats and fine wine. You can eat anything if you're a lady and the ship's named for you."

"Where does everyone else eat?" Hannah asked.

"Why, we eat wherever convenient on the main deck or sometimes on the spar deck above. Each family cooks its own meal on little charcoal fires set in boxes of sand."

Hannah felt confused by so much information. How could she remember everything? "Do you think we can find my family now?"

"Follow me," Zach replied. He led her down a steep, narrow set of steps that was almost like a ladder that entered below the floor. It was so dark, she could barely see. She wondered how she would ever be able to make out the maze of ladders, dark recesses, and unlit passages. How many decks were down here?

"The trick," Zach said over his shoulder to her, "is to count the steps from the quarterdeck to the upper deck, from the upper deck to the gun deck. That way your feet find their own way."

Hannah only felt more perplexed and lost. People tugging enormous chests pushed past. Grown men stooped so as not to bump their heads against the low ceiling. Babies cried. She heard women's voices arguing over cooking fires. "Who took my biscuits? Did thou?"

Powerful smells nearly made Hannah dizzy. Every deck seam oozed with tar. Every mast and spar was sticky with resin. Every stay and halyard dripped with pitch. Hannah wondered if she might be sick. But she did not want to embarrass herself in front of Zach. She tried not to breathe through her nose.

"This is the lower deck," Zach announced. "Here you'll find the guns secured for sea. If we meet with Dunkirkers, the guns can be rolled quickly into place."

"Dunkirkers?"

"Pirates."

"Oh," Hannah said nervously. "And what are those?" She pointed to the strange spiderweblike nets hanging from the low ceiling.

"Sailors' beds. They're called hammocks, and they swing down and rock like babies' cradles when the ship moves," Zach explained.

Hannah held her nose. "What's that awful smell?"

"Bilge water," Zach replied. "Waste and other garbage mixes with leaking seawater and ballast—sand and gravel in the very bottom of the ship's hold that keeps it from tipping. Doesn't smell much worse than the London sewers. Don't worry, you'll get used to it."

Hannah walked faster. She didn't think she'd ever grow accustomed to the awful odor.

"I heard a sailor say this is a sweet ship," Zach continued. "Carried only wine from the Mediterranean. The other ships trading in fish and worse stink to high heaven. Nobody thought of Saints traveling overseas. Come this way."

Darkness seemed even more overwhelming in the hold. A few candles burned. "This is where the goods are kept. The food storage. Fifteen thousand brown biscuits of the common sort and five thousand white biscuits made with sweet and good wheat. There's thirty hogsheads of salt horse."

"What's salt horse?"

"Salted beef. Plus six hogsheads of pork and two hundred neats tongue—nearly twelve thousand pounds of meat."

Hannah looked about the mountains of barrels and crates and beer casks. It looked like enough food to feed everyone for a year. "How do you know so much about the food?"

Zach winked. "I was here when the ship was loaded. I'm very good at listening and being invisible."

"What are thou rascally children doing in here?" came a loud angry voice. "Be gone. This area's not for the likes of you!"

"The cook! Run!" shouted Zach.

Desperately Hannah tried to keep up with

him as he dodged about the salt barrels, the butter firkins, and bushels of peas and oatmeal. The cook swung a meat cleaver, but Hannah and Zach managed to scramble up the ladder unharmed.

Hannah slumped breathlessly against a wall as two children dashed past in a game of hide-and-seek. "I want my family. Where are they?"

"No harm done. Right this way," said Zach. He did not look the least upset.

Perhaps he's used to running away from meat cleavers. Hannah followed him into the 'tween decks. There she heard Abigail's voice. She ran to the corner where she found her sister unpacking clothing from their enormous trunk. A moan came from the pallet next to the wall.

"Hannah, where have you been?" Abigail demanded. "You missed prayers. Goody Garrett is sick. Father has gone for fresh water to bathe her face."

"I was trying to find you," Hannah insisted. She looked over her shoulder. Zach had vanished.

"Who was that boy?" Abigail asked.

Hannah sighed. *No escape.* "His name is Zach."

Abigail's eyes narrowed. "I fear he is a Stranger."

"What does that mean?" Hannah asked.

"He is not one of God's Children."

"How can you tell? You don't know everything."

Abigail gave her younger sister a withering look. "Father will not be pleased."

Hannah sat on a bundle of clothing. Her shoulders hunched forward.

"You are every moment in God's hands. His eye is always upon you. Don't ever forget that." Abigail adjusted a blanket over Goody Garrett.

Hannah pulled her damp cloak around her shoulders. She reached into her pocket and felt the hidden thunderbolt. Slowly she rubbed her thumb along the cool, smooth edge and thought how much she missed Caleb.

My Record of Remarkables

March 20, 1630

I struggle mightily to endure many injustices, oh Lord grant me Patience. These many days we have been *Waiting to Begin our Journey. We sailed down the Thames on our ship, the* Arbella. *The whole Time I kept Hannah beside me on deck and did not allow her to Explore the ship or Wander from my Sight. It was a swift journey and the Curious Child did not get into any Innocent Mischief because as soon as we arrived in Southampton, we left the ship and found lodging on shore. Our stepmother refuses to stay on board for Fear of Unhealthful Air in the harbor. This great luxury of lodging on shore Dear Father does not Protest, though well he should for it costs him Plenty. As he is very Busy with planning and Seeing to our luggage and Provisions, Hannah and I have had to Endure our Stepmother's unkind orders, which I strive to Obey.*

Yesterday she gave to me a letter to be delivered in great haste to the nearest post for Chelmsford. She told me not to look upon it or show it to Dear Father but to carry it swiftly, which I did. But I confess I did Look upon it and Discovered it was Addressed to my brother. This I found Odd. Satan whispered in my Ear and said 'Open it and Read therein,' but I did not. And although I considered destroying the Letter, I carried it as she wished. I drew strength from the Reverend

Hooker's words: "A Christian's great Care should be to keep the Heart pure."

Once we came on board the **Arbella**, I soon discovered that not all the travelers are Holy people. Some I fear are using the ship to Escape from Lives of Crime and Sin. I pray for them.

My sister must be Watched constantly. Belowdecks we have Less Privacy than that which we are accustomed. Our foul-smelling sleeping area between the decks has pallets crowded everywhere on the floor and hammocks hung from every point of vantage. Our Stepmother in her present Perilous Condition insisted that Dear Father hang a blanket around our tiny sleeping area (for he must sleep in a hammock). But this partition can not block the smells of spewing and sounds of sickness all around us. Our Stepmother is quite ill from the dancing of the ship, and I must bathe her forehead constant though she never thanks me for my Troubles even though I am not well myself.

Please God help me temper my impatience. I resolve never to allow the least measure of any fretting or uneasiness for my Dear Father and our demanding stepmother, who is a cross I must bear.

Chapter 4

Deare loving Brother Caleb at Chelmsford:

I hope that this shall come safe to your
hands. You may be surprised to hear that
we have still not left England's shore but
ride at anchor near a place called Yarmouth.
The wind! We wait for the right wind and
sometimes I think it will never come. Very
tempestuous weather blows at us from the
southwest, Father says, and blocks our
departure these many days. I asked him
why we do not go another direction to
America but he says No there is only one
direction for us now and the wind must

push us through the Needles. I know not
what he means. Does it not sound very difficult for a such a large ship to fit through the
eye of a needle? We spied a ship from
Holland twice our size wrecked along the
shore, crushed and crawling with poor
sailors trying to save their lives. They looked
small as ants. God save them. I wish I knew
how to swim. I am lonely these days because
Abigail is so sick and cannot play with me.
The ship dances in this stormy weather and
she spews and does not rise from her bed.
Father is sick, too, and so is Goody Garrett.
I have not been sick. I stay above deck as
much as I can because the smell is not so
awful, tho the air is cold and biting.

In the *Talbot* I heard a woman was lately
delivered of a son. I wonder what it would
be like to be born on a boat. There are many
children skylarking about in the rigging,
playing hide-and-seek. As soon as the
Reverend Phillips is well enough, he will
give us catechism lessons. We shant neglect
our studies after all. Abigail is pleased. I

confess I am not. Did you know all ships are called She because of tradition? Father told me a ship can be as moody and difficult as a woman. Do you think women are moody and difficult? I must close and hope that God will forgive all my faults. Commend my blessing to Grandmother. This may be my last letter to you. Keep us in your prayers.

> Your lovinge sister,
> Hannah
> Aboard the *Arbella* riding
> before Yarmouth
> April 1, 1630

On the first fair morning in nearly a week, Hannah sat on the ship's deck in a sunny spot out of the wind. Abigail, Father, and Goody Garrett were still too sick to leave their beds. "I charge you to pray daily and read your Bible and fear to sin," Father told her. Obediently she had brought her Bible to study. But across the way she could hear laughter. She closed the Bible and crept closer.

She was surprised to discover two girls wearing green velvet masks, the kind designed to keep harmful sun from fair, well-bred faces. *What kind of children are these?* On their hands the girls wore embroidered silk gloves. Dainty lace fell from their wrists. The taller girl wore a soft gray cloak lined with yellow satin. Around her neck was a lace-edged ruff, a stiff, pleated collar that reminded Hannah of a platter. The younger girl looked to be perhaps eight years old. Like her companion, she wore a fine soft gray cloak that was open enough to reveal the yellow-and-black stripes of her taffeta skirt.

The girls took no notice of Hannah. They sat facing each other, striking each others' hands and then their own knees while chanting:

> "*Pease porridge hot,*
> *Pease porridge cold,*
> *Pease porridge in the pot,*
> *Nine days old.*"

Hannah chimed in without missing a beat, "Some like it hot, some like it cold, some like it in the pot nine days old." She smiled. "May I play, too?"

The older girl removed her mask, revealing a pale, proud face with a long nose and dark eyes. "Who art thou?"

"Hannah Garrett of Chelmsford."

"And who is your father?" the younger girl spoke up. She, too, removed her velvet mask. She gazed quizzically at Hannah with blue, eager eyes. Her face was thin and delicate.

"My father is a shoemaker, miss," Hannah said and curtsied. The girls laughed. Hannah felt encouraged. *They think I'm funny.* "May I . . . may I play?" she asked again. *Certainly Abigail will not criticize these finely dressed girls as friends. They do not look the least like raggedy Zach.*

"I'm not sure we require thou to play with us," the older girl said and sniffed. She slipped her mask back in place so that Hannah could no longer see her haughty expression.

"Oh, Rosamond," the younger girl whined, "let her join us. She may be amusing."

"All right, Grace," Rosamond said in a bored

voice. She examined Hannah. "What games do you know to entertain us? Something to give us warmth on such a cold day."

Hannah had to think fast. She glanced quickly about the deck and spied a rope. She stretched the rope so that it lay straight. She tied one end of the rope to the grate near the hatchway that led down into the hold. "Do you know the Darby jig?" she asked.

Rosamond shook her head. "We are not allowed to dance."

"It's not a dance," Hannah replied. "It's a jumping game. You hop and skip very quickly from one side of the rope to the other."

"Show us!" Grace commanded.

Hannah stood with one foot on one side of the rope, the other foot on the other. She placed her hands on her hips and hoisted her skirt slightly so that her feet would be free to move quickly. She took a deep breath and hopped and skipped as she sang.

> *"Darby, darby, jig, jig, jig,*
> *I've been to bed with a big, big wig!*

I went to France to learn to dance—
Darby, darby, jig, jig, jig!"

Grace and Rosamond giggled. "Bravo!" Rosamond said gaily. "May I try?" She rose elegantly and joined Hannah in the same pose. She straddled the rope, lifting her skirt ever so slightly so that her ankles covered with sky blue stockings showed.

"Darby, darby, jig, jig, jig,
I've been to bed with a big, big wig!
I went to France to learn to dance—
Darby, darby, jig, jig, jig!"

"'Tis my turn now!" Grace cried. "Only faster this time. Rosamond, you are too slow." Grace danced up and down the rope back and forth while Rosamond and Hannah sang and clapped. When she twirled, her full skirt swished. She spun with her arms outstretched, as if eager to outdo her sister. "Look at me!" she cried. "'Darby, darby, jig, jig, jig . . .'"

"Take care!" Rosamond shouted.

Grace danced faster and faster like someone unaccustomed to so much freedom of movement. She careened wildly toward the edge of the hatchway opening, lurched headfirst, and vanished.

Hannah watched, stunned. She was unable to move, unable to speak. Rosamond let out an ear-piercing scream.

"What's the matter?" a man's deep, commanding voice demanded.

"Father, Grace has fallen!" Rosamond cried. She motioned tearfully toward the open hatchway that led deep into the cook room and then to the hold.

Before Rosamond's father could rush down the ladder, a bellow echoed from below. "Make way!" A red-haired sailor climbed up the ladder with Grace over one shoulder. He hoisted her on to the deck as if she were no heavier than a firkin of butter. Grace looked about dazed, but unhurt. "I caught this creature flying down into the cook's room," the sailor said, not the least bit surprised. "Nary a scratch on her."

Grace's father gathered his little daughter up in his arms. "Praise be to God!"

"And *my* nimbleness, sir. My name is Peaches, sir," the sailor said.

Grace's father only sniffed with contempt.

Peaches turned away, muttering, "Turd in all your teeth!"

Hannah gasped when she caught a glimpse of his fiery face. *The man from the London alleyway!*

"Rosamond, what wild carelessness was this that caused your sister to nearly fall to her death?" the girls' father demanded.

"Father, the accident was all *her* fault." Rosamond pointed to Hannah.

Hannah trembled and curtsied.

"Who art thou?" he demanded. "Did thou push her?"

"Hannah Garrett, your worship. And, no, sir, I did not. We were playing a game. A harmless jumping game. Grace fell."

"Does thou know who I am?" he asked. "Does thou know who these young ladies are?"

"No, your worship."

"I am Sir Saltonstall. And these are my daughters."

Hannah gulped. *Am I to be hanged?* Sir Saltonstall was far above her father's station. He was a gentleman and a knight.

"Here, here. What commotion is this?" demanded a sallow-faced man in a sad-colored cloak. He had a beaked nose and thinning hair.

"John Winthrop," Sir Saltonstall replied, "is it not enough on this voyage that we have faced inexcusable, endless delays and mysterious disappearances of dozens of our best white biscuits? Why do you allow ruffians and romping, ungodly children on this ship to tempt and torment my sensitive daughters?"

Wearily Winthrop listened to the details of the accident. He laced and unlaced his long, pale fingers in front of his chest. He rocked back on his heels with his eyes half-shut. "I think, Sir Saltonstall, we should thank Providence that your daughter was not injured. Only for the incredible swiftness of Captain Milborne's seaman was she saved from irreparable harm. As for you, child," he said, turning to Hannah, "I suggest you seek your own kind. Be dutiful and respectful. Be humble, modest, womanly, and discreet."

Hannah nodded and curtsied.

"You may never play or associate with my daughters again," Sir Saltonstall added. Rosamond gave Hannah a withering look.

Hannah curtsied again. But this time she had to blink back tears. Now she knew what it felt like to be unjustly unwanted. *Like Zach.* Then she had another horrible thought. *What will Father do when he finds out?*

"Let us pray and thank God for his goodness," Winthrop intoned. Everyone bent their heads in prayer. Hannah glanced secretly at the sailor. He did not pray. He folded his arms in front of himself and rolled his eyes.

"Stay not among the wicked, Peaches!" a sailor crowed from the rigging in mocking singsong. "'Lest that with them you perish. But let us to New England go, and the pagan people cherish!'"

A nearby crowd of sailors roared oaths and hooted. "That," Winthrop announced, "is quite —"

Suddenly a cry went up from high in the rigging. "Dunkirkers ahead!"

American Sisters

"Pirates!" Winthrop said grimly. "Get your family to safety, Sir Saltonstall."

For once Sir Saltonstall followed someone else's order without complaint. The ship swarmed with activity. "Clear the decks!" Captain Milborne shouted. "Make ready the powder chests and guns!"

Hannah knew she had to get back to her family below. Yet she dreaded going back into the hold again. *I'll miss everything.* She lingered on the deck, watching sailors rush past with rolled hammocks and powder chests and piles of muskets. When she peered into the distance, she could make out the ominous shape of eight ships coming directly their way.

"Get below! All women and children below!" shouted the captain. "Dismantle the cabins on the gun deck! Make ready the cannons."

The ladies housed on the quarterdeck were quickly ushered toward the hold for protection. Their makeshift cabins constructed on the gun deck were quickly pried apart and dismantled so that more space could be given for men to aim muskets and cannons.

"Well, I never!" Lady Arbella announced. She flapped her black fan and carefully lowered herself out of sight into the hold.

"Eight ships to our mere four," a familiar voice said. "I would not call that sporting odds."

Hannah turned and saw Zach. Unlike everyone else on deck, Zach was smiling from ear to ear. "Can't wait for the fighting to begin. Hand-to-hand combat! Leaping ship to ship! Such excitement!"

Hannah looked at Zach in astonishment. "What are you saying? You can't fight without asking permission of your master. What will he say?"

"Who cares what Master Pyncheon thinks?" Zach replied with a shrug of his shoulders. "If he says I can't fight, I'll run away and join the pirates."

Hannah felt someone grip her elbow. Zach rose slightly off the ground as he was picked up by the back of his collar. "We said get below. Now get!" a sailor growled. He shoved Hannah and Zach roughly in the direction of the hold. Reluctantly Zach followed Hannah down the ladder to join the company of weeping women and howling children.

In the twilight of the hold, Hannah made her way carefully. "Goodbye. Good luck," Hannah called to Zach, who moved expertly among the boxes and trunks and bundles to find his master. After much stumbling, Hannah finally located her family. "Where have you been?" Abigail demanded.

She didn't see. She hasn't heard. Hannah felt relieved. Neither Abigail nor anyone else in her family had learned of her encounter with Sir Saltonstall. *With the arrival of pirates, who cares about such a foolish accident?*

"What is happening?" Father asked weakly. "What is that booming noise?"

"Cannons. Pirates in eight ships are approaching," Hannah said in her most helpful voice. "I saw them."

Goody Garrett groaned. Father lifted his head from his bed. "We must pray for deliverance."

After the family prayed, Hannah watched with satisfaction as Grace and her sister huddled atop a sea chest several yards away. In the grim darkness of the hold, Sir Saltonstall's daughters had no need for green velvet masks. Rosamond held a dirty wooden bucket in her dainty gloved hands and spewed as loudly as any commoner.

My Record of Remarkables

Oh, Lord take away my Terrible sickness! Even the conserve of Wormwood Dear Father gave me does no good. My spirit is excessively broken and I fear there is Danger of my Dying suddenly with Griefs and Fears. . . . Protect my sister in my absence. . . .

Chapter

5

Dearest brother Caleb at Chelmsford:

I must be brief. It is my hope that one
day you will find this and be able to cipher
my strange scribble. I can barely see as I
write. My only light comes from the main
hatch grating above. All women and children and feeble or sick passengers have
been forced to stay below these past twelve
hours as our captain and crew readies for a
fight. Wild rumors fill us with dread. Some
say eight enemy ships are only one league
away. Abigail and Goody Garrett pray and
weep. Only Father remains brave. If the

pirates kill all of us, know that I remain your devoted sister even after Death. We are all given to God: and there I am, and love to be.

    Your ever affectionate sister,

> Hannah aboard the *Arbella*
> April 9, 1630

                ❧

"What was that noise?" Hannah whispered in the crowded darkness belowdecks.

"My arm! Must you grab it so tight every time you hear a noise?" Abigail said wearily. "That sound was just more gunshots. Maybe target practice again."

Hannah held her nose. Even so, she still felt surrounded by the odor of wet wool, urine, spoiled food, vomit, and unwashed bodies.

Abigail stroked Hannah's back. "Why not get some rest?"

"Can't. I'm too afraid."

Footsteps drummed loudly on the deck above. Muffled shouts. Then the heavy grinding noise of cannon wheels. Nervously Hannah slipped her hand inside her pocket and held the thunderbolt. More footsteps crashed overhead.

Goody Garrett moaned. "What news?"

"Nothing, my dear," Father murmured.

"Huzza! Huzza!" came a sudden resounding cheer.

"What are they saying?" one of the passengers called.

Someone screamed. "They've boarded the ship!"

"Be still!"

"We'll all be killed!"

The hatchway was thrown open and the hold flooded with a bright square of sunlight. Hannah and her sister clung to each other in the shadows—silent, expecting the worst. The thundering boots of murderous pirates.

"Hallo!" cried Peaches. "Captain says you can come up. The ships are friends. Our danger is over."

A loud cheer went up among the people in the hold. Hannah jumped up and grabbed her sister's hands and twirled Abigail around and around—not caring who they bumped into.

Above deck a cannon fired. Several rounds of muskets went off.

"God be praised!" Father said.

Goody Garrett clasped her slender hands together. "We are saved."

Hannah scrambled up the hatchway with Abigail close behind. She passed Peaches, who stood ready to help passengers up on to the deck. "Thanks to thee," Hannah said to him, certain God was watching.

"For what, miss?" Peaches replied. "You just climbed up that ladder on your own two feet."

"Thanks to thee for catching Sir Saltonstall's daughter."

"Ah," said Peaches. With a wave of his hand he dismissed the entire rescue.

"Come on, Hannah!" Abigail cried. "Over here!"

The girls watched the large ships approaching. Like the *Arbella*, the ships signaled with friendly fire, their flags unfurled. The passengers waved their hats and handkerchiefs, delighted to welcome friends.

Meanwhile, the *Arbella*'s crew was busy

adjusting sails and rigging and lowering the anchor. Peaches told Hannah that a long boat was being lowered from the *Neptune,* one of the eight ships on its way back from Canada and Newfoundland. A second long boat containing three large barrels was launched with six sailors pulling hard at the oars. "See how low she rides in the water?" Peaches said.

Hannah peered over the side and watched the heavy, gray-bearded captain of the *Neptune* climb aboard the *Arbella.*

"Who are those others he's bringing?" Abigail asked.

Hannah craned her neck and spotted three dark-haired people huddled at one end of the boat.

"Perhaps some high-up officers," Peaches said before he vanished.

Hannah moved closer so that she could better hear and see the new arrivals.

"We are returning from a most profitable voyage," Captain Endecott said in a most jovial manner, "and offer you the opportunity to purchase excellent fresh fish of diverse sorts."

Captain Endecott shook hands with Captain Milborne, who looked as if he were very relieved not to be greeting a pirate.

Captain Milborne made a short bow. "And who are the other passengers you've brought with you?"

The three strangers clambered on board with iron shackles on their legs. As they walked, the heavy iron made a harsh clanging sound. Hannah had never seen such dark skin, dark eyes, dark hair. *Arbella's* passengers crowded around.

"Devils!" one woman whispered fearfully.

"Heathens," the Reverend Phillips said with pious authority. "Savages have no souls."

"Thou Saints have strange ideas," Captain Endecott said and laughed. "These are Pawtucket from Agawam. That's what the Indian who sold them to us said. You folks get to see them for free. We're bringing them back to London. Crowds will pay a good price to see a curiosity from the New World."

Hannah stared in bafflement at the dark man with the proud, distant eyes. He looked at no one. But the woman and the girl gazed panic-stricken about the ship. The woman was scantily dressed in a ragged skirt and an oversize sailor's coat. Beside her cowered the young girl. Her filthy, dark hair lay matted against her thin face. Dressed in a coarse tunic, the girl shivered from the cold, but did not bother to wipe her runny nose. She wore no shoes. Her ankles were raw and festering where the great iron shackles rubbed.

"I don't like the looks of them," a woman said in a shrill voice. "See how that one gives the evil eye?"

"Captain, are they dangerous?" a man asked.

Captain Endecott shook his head. "No, but they would escape if they could—even though it's nearly three thousand miles back to their own shore."

"Passengers, be on your way. There's nothing more to see here," Captain Milborne said with obvious irritation. "Captain Endecott, come to my cabin for some refreshment. I want to hear news of your voyage. The rest of you, go back to your own business."

Captain Milborne left two armed soldiers to lounge nearby the three curiosities bound for London. Little by little, the grown-ups dispersed to cook a hot meal or catch an hour of sleep. Free at last, the children of the *Arbella* ran and leaped about the deck, exhilarated by the sunshine and fresh air.

"Come away," Abigail said, pulling Hannah by her arm. "Those heathens are devilish looking and not to be trusted."

Hannah stared at the shackled girl. "She is no older than I."

"So?" Abigail replied impatiently.

"See how she shivers from the cold? Why does no one offer anything for her to wear? Why does no one offer anything for her to eat?"

Abigail rolled her eyes in disgust. "Because she is not human. Neither are the other two. Let us away."

Hannah refused to budge. "They are very like us. Don't you see?"

"If the Reverend Phillips should hear you talk," Abigail hissed, "he would make you understand. What do you mean by such dangerous nonsense?"

"They are on a long, dangerous voyage," Hannah said softly, "to a place they have never been before—just like us. No wonder they look so frightened."

"Those fumes in the hold must have damaged your brain!" Abigail exploded. "You know very well that heathens are nothing like you and I. They are damned. They will surely burn in hell. Come away before you say anything else you will regret." With great vigor, Abigail pulled her unwilling sister to the other end of the ship—out of sight of the Pawtucket. Even so, Hannah could not shake from her mind the image of the shivering girl's terrified eyes.

My Record of Remarkables

April 10, 1630

God's great mercy Delivers us! It is our good fortune to have found ourselves in the Company of Friends, not Pirate enemies! I must meditate on the experience I have of God's faithfulness and goodness I have

*had. . . . I shall make a catalog of God's special
providences:*

. . . Upon smelling the fresh breeze over the waves

. . . Upon seeing the brilliant blue sky

. . . Upon hearing the splash of gentle waves

*Even the loud calling sea birds have their satisfactions!
Oh! the Glory, oh, the glorious Joy of their Goodness!*

*I am determined to be well so that I can celebrate all
of God's wonders. And so that I may continue to watch
over my Sister, who, in my absence, has fallen in with
bad Company. I must help her see the Error of her Ways.*

*Three ignorant captured savages were brought on
board and left on display by another captain while he
visited our ship. When I saw them, I recalled that
Christ hath said blessed are the merciful for ye shall
obtain mercy. And so, when no one was looking, I crept
up to these poor lost souls bound for Hell and I read to
them from the Bible. The man savage spat on me. But I
did not give up. "You must not think to go to heaven on
a feather bed," Reverend Hook told us. "If you will be
Christ's disciples, you must take up his cross; and it
will make you sweat." So I persisted in reading More
Holy Words. And the woman and girl seemed to listen
and perhaps to understand something of God's goodness,*

for when I finished and gave them each a dipperful of water and a biscuit, they smiled and there was tears out of their eyes just like ordinary human tears. And I hoped for their conversion.

Oh! How I pray one day people will say of me: "She had a Strange Sweetness in her mind, and singular purity in her Affections; she was most just and conscientious in all her conduct; no one could persuade her to do anything wrong or Sinful."

When one of the foul sailors chased me from the Savages, I prayed for him, too.

The next day the wind shifted to the northeast. Farewell was quickly said to Captain Endecott. The *Neptune* and the other ships went on their way. Sails were raised and the *Arbella* headed out to sea in a handsome gale and fair weather. Hannah stood at the railing and looked back toward land. In the distance she could just make out a strange rocky shape.

"That's called the Lizard."

Hannah jumped at the sound of Zach's voice. "How do you know?" she asked, surprised that she felt glad to see him.

"Peaches told me. He said it's the southern-most tip of Cornwall. The last we'll see of England."

"Farewell then, Caleb," Hannah murmured sadly.

"Who's Caleb?"

"My brother." Hannah patted her pocket to make sure the thunderbolt was still safe.

Zach peered into the distance. "I haven't got anybody left over there. I don't care if I never set foot in England again."

"Never?"

"Never. After I arrive in America and serve my time as a servant, I intend to make my fortune and be a free man." Zach leaned on the railing with one elbow, his chin in his palm. He stared down into the roiling waves and was silent for several moments.

Hannah stared at the water, too. *Be a free man? What strange talk is this? A servant is a servant all his life.* She cleared her throat and decided to change the subject. "I've heard there are plenty of big fish down there."

"Some are as enormous as a house," Zach

replied. "Some are wider and longer than a ship. Some can swim and fly through the air. Others spout huge fountains of water."

Hannah gave Zach a quick sideways stare. *Is he lying again?* But his face looked perfectly serious. "I would like to see such a great fish."

"I'm sure you will," Zach said mysteriously. "The ocean is filled with many wonders. Did you hear about the time some Essex fishermen caught a wild man in their nets?"

"No," said Hannah nervously. "What happened?"

"They took him to Orford Castle and locked him up. The wild man was entirely naked and like a human being in all his limbs. He had hair, though it was mostly torn away and nearly destroyed. His beard was full and pointed and his chest was extremely hairy and shaggy."

Hannah bit her fingernails, even though Abigail forbade it. "Did the wild man die?"

Zach solemnly shook his head. "The knight at Orford Castle guarded the wild man day and night for a long time. He did not let him approach the sea."

Hannah thought again of the hungry Pawtucket girl. "What did they feed the wild man?"

"Fish raw as well as cooked. When he was served raw fish, he wrung out the fish with his hands so that all the liquid was gone." Zach demonstrated by making a twisting motion with his hands. "He ate very greedily, you can be sure."

"Did he have a name?" Hannah asked.

Zach shrugged. "No one knew. You see, he would not utter a word. Even when they hung him upside down by his feet and severely tortured him. They tried to take him to a church. But he would not pray or kneel or bow his head. Instead, he hurried to his sleeping place in the castle and hid until the next morning."

Hannah felt a shiver run down her spine. "Do you suppose," she whispered, "he was a devil?"

"Hannah, what's this idle chatter?" Abigail demanded. She looked at Zach's shabby leather jerkin and unraveling blue yarn stockings. She sniffed. "Thou smells of bilge, Stranger."

"You don't smell so sweetly yourself, Saint," Zach said and tipped his hat.

Hannah hid her smile with her hand.

"I can see you have been biting your finger-nails again," Abigail said.

Hannah concealed her hand inside her cloak.

"Come away from this rude ruffian, Hannah," Abigail commanded. "Now that I'm finally well enough to come up on deck, sit with me and sew."

"I don't want to sit and sew. I want to hear the rest of Zach's story." Hannah looked out over the waves, hoping to spot an enormous spouting fish or a wild man. When she glanced back at her sister, she saw her hurt expression.

"Do as you wish," Abigail replied. She turned and stomped away, her head held high.

Hannah sighed. She knew her sister would make her life very unbearable the rest of the day.

"Now there's a Miss Prat-A-Pace," Zach said. "Does she always bark at you like that?"

Hannah felt confused and embarrassed. She had never talked to anyone else about the way her sister treated her. "Sometimes," she said slowly, "Abigail is very nice to me."

Zach did not look the least convinced. "I should rather have no sister or brother than to have one so fearsome and bossy. Don't look sad, Hannah. Would you like to hear the rest of the story?"

Hannah nodded eagerly.

"Where was I?"

"Hiding in the castle until dawn."

"Once," Zach said in a low, confidential tone, "the men from the castle took the wild man down to the harbor and let him loose in the sea after securing a triple line of very stout nets across the harbor. But the wild man soon made for the depths of the sea, passing all the nets. Over and over the wild man would come up from the deep water and gaze at those watching him from shore for a very long time. Then he'd dive down and reappear after a moment, as though he was mocking those men whose strongest nets could not hold him."

"Did he escape?" Hannah asked.

"He did not. And that's the wonder of it. He played like this in the sea for a long while. Everyone thought he'd never come back. But he did. He swam through the waves and remained at the castle for two more months. During this time, he was not so heavily guarded. No one knew how much he disliked his new way of life. And one day he secretly slipped down to the sea and never appeared again."

"Was he a mortal man?"

Zach drummed the railing with his long, dirty fingers. "He might have been a fish pretending to be a human being. He might have been an evil spirit lurking in the body of a drowned man. No one ever knew for sure."

Hannah shivered. She looked out over the constant movement of white caps. Even now, hidden in the dancing water, someone might be watching her.

My Record of Remarkables

April 11, 1630

I have many faults. I see the virtues of a few and look down with contempt on the general run. I am wanting in real fortitude, though nothing is so useful.

I fear my sister has ruined our Family's good Name.

Could I have somehow helped her avoid such Untoward Contact with Sir Saltonstall's daughters? What Devil visited her thus that I might have prevented?

My stepmother Cries and Laments as we leave sight of England for good. I try to console her as best I can.

Think how this baby will be born in the new Zion, I tell her. That will be a great happiness, will it not?

Still she cries as if her heart would break.

I cannot but guess who she so sorely misses.

Chapter 6

Dearest Brother Caleb at Chelmsford:

My humble duty remembered to you. I know not when this letter may reach England, but I write all the same because it gives me comfort. We are still alive, thanks be to God. No pirates attacked as we feared. Reverend Phillips celebrated with a most inspiring long sermon, tho the sailors did not think so and showed no respect. They jeered and mocked and made profane noises that upset Father and the others. I tried my best to listen carefully but my mind wandered. Do you think I am as terrible as

Abigail says? Father, too, is angry at me because I smirched our family's good name. All because of a clumsy daughter of a gentleman. I begged his forgiveness and I shall never play with her again. I know that I have a great many imperfections and that it will require time and patience to cure them. I do not think I have a bad temper, but, on the contrary, very good. My heart is open to warm impressions and I am very affectionate. But Abigail says I have a bold forwardness, which is disgusting. You oppose all restraint with too much vigor, she told me. You tell your opinions and think them better than those of other people who are wiser than you. Do you think I have no mildness in my character? I must close and hide this as it is time for prayers again.

> Your loving sister unto death,
> Hannah
> April 10, 1630

The next day the masts vanished upward into nothing in the cold, drifting fog. Hannah could see her breath. She tilted her head back and gazed skyward. Overhead, invisible canvas flapped and banged aimlessly. When she looked over the railing, the horizon and most of the ocean had disappeared as well. No wind. The *Arbella* floated motionless, shrouded in thick mist.

To her amazement, two legs suddenly clambered down the rigging, then a blue coat, arms, a head. "Ahoy, miss!" Peaches said, grinning. His hair appeared even more brilliant against the pale fog. "You look like you seen a ghost."

Hannah shut her gaping mouth. "Where did thou come from?"

"The ratlines," Peaches said, jutting his stubby thumb skyward. "Had to creep up to the foretop. Though setting sails won't do much good. We're not going anywhere without a hatful of wind." Peaches took his pipe from his pocket and lit it. His hands were raw and cut from hauling rigging. He crouched on a coil of rope on deck as easily and comfortably as if it were a soft arm chair in a proper house. "Some seamen say they can whistle for a wind. Others claim how a fellow sets his cap brings the wind back. But the surest way I know is to stick a knife in the mast. That never fails to bring the wind round again."

Hannah glanced nervously into the impenetrable shroud of fog. "Can thou tell which way we're headed in such weather?"

Peaches blew a ring of acrid smoke. "No, miss. Not in such a stinking fog as this. Our biggest danger isn't getting lost."

Hannah breathed a sigh of relief.

"Our biggest danger," Peaches continued, "is running afoul of the three ships following us. Or smashing up against a stray iceberg."

Boom! Boom-a-boom!

Hannah jumped. "What was that?"

"Warning shots from the *Talbot* or the *Jewel* or the *Ambrose* to tell us where they are." Peaches stood up and stretched. "Would you like to help with her answer?"

Hannah nodded, though she felt confused. *What does he mean—"her answer?"*

Peaches disappeared for a few moments, then returned with a large drum. "You look like a very strong, helpful sort. Give it a go, miss." He handed her a large drumstick.

Hannah beat the drum as hard as she could. *Bumpa-bumpa-bump!* The hollow sound was very satisfying and very loud. "Can the other ships hear us and tell where we are?"

Peaches smiled. "Let's hope so. Drum away."

Hannah beat the drum for the next hour while Peaches relit his pipe and relaxed on the coil of rope again. Every so often he would give her words of encouragement. "Fine job, miss. You're a regular sailor."

Stubborn fog and dead calm wore on for a second day. Tempers aboard ship soon began to flare.

"Why are those two men's hands tied thus?" Abigail demanded. She and Hannah sat on deck with sewing in their laps. They watched two scowling fellows from Sussex marching past with their hands tied behind their backs.

"Father said they were caught in a fistfight,"

Hannah said. "They must walk together back and forth till nightfall. That is their punishment."

Something dark and furry and small dashed boldly across the deck and disappeared among some barrels. "What was that?" Hannah asked. Instinctively she jumped to her feet and held her arms close to herself as if for protection.

"Rats are everywhere nibbling away," Abigail said and sighed. She took another stitch. "You should see what they did to the lovely Cheshire cheese Father brought. Gnawed away the whole thing in less than an hour's time."

"Not the good cheese!" Hannah said and sat down.

"And then they ate an enormous keeping cake. The only food the rats have left us are the cakes that Grandmother made."

"Those strong, flat grayish objects she decorated with calcined raisins?" Hannah said and groaned. "I wish they'd eaten *those* instead. I never even had a taste of the cheese before it vanished."

"Speaking of mysterious disappearances, have

you seen my favorite thimble? The silver one. I cannot find it and now I must search everywhere. Did you take it?"

"I did not," Hannah replied. She squinted as she bent over the stocking she was footing. Even in the middle of the day, the lack of sun gave everything a dim, shadowy appearance.

Abigail pouted. "I cannot find it. And now I will have to search everywhere."

"Let us not sew anymore," Hannah said, hoping to cheer her sister. "Tell dreams instead. Put out your hands—

> *"Ikamy, dukkamy, alligar, mole,*
> *Dick slew alligar slum . . ."*

"Come on. What's wrong? Why aren't you playing?"

"I do not have any dreams worth telling."

"What about a story? Tell a story."

"I cannot think of any stories as exciting as that boy's."

Hannah took a deep breath. "He has a name. It's Zachariah Punt."

Abigail wrinkled her nose. "What kind of name is that?"

Hannah scowled and stood up. *How she does provoke me!* "I am tired of sitting. These rats make me nervous. Come for a walk around on the deck."

"I am perfectly fine where I am." Abigail straightened the pleats of her soiled petticoat.

Hannah hurried away, struggling with all her might not to imagine beating her sister with a stick the way she had beaten the drum. *Bump-a-bump-a!* She smiled, then winced. *I must not think unkindly of Abigail.* She repeated this over and over as she swung her arms and circled around the main mast past a group of children playing cat's cradle. She surveyed the group, hoping to catch sight of Zach. He was nowhere to be seen.

From the quarterdeck came the sound of voices. "Captain Milborne, my good white biscuits are missing," Master Pyncheon complained in a loud, piercing voice. "We were promised five pounds a person of salt beef, pork, salt fish, butter, cheese, pease pottage, water gruel, good biscuits, and six shillings beer. Does thou know where my biscuits are? I have paid more than my share on this voyage for myself and my servant. I demand satisfaction. Where are my biscuits?"

With a stony-faced expression, Captain Milborne folded his arms in front of his chest. "Eaten by rats. Lost overboard. How should I know? See to the purser. I have much bigger problems to worry about than your bread ration."

"Sir," Master Pyncheon repeated, louder this time, "I am an Essex yeoman with extensive land holdings and furnishings and—"

"I don't care who you are, you easily kindled chimney," Captain Milborne interrupted. "I am the captain. This is my ship. You will do as I say. Get off my quarterdeck."

Back in Chelmsford, no one would dare speak that way to someone as powerful as Master Pyncheon, but aboard ship there were new rules, new masters. Defeated, Master Pyncheon scowled and slunk down the stairway. *How Zach would have enjoyed this spectacle!* Hannah tried her best to keep from grinning.

"Hello, Hannah!" Zach called. He waved to her from across the deck. Hunched beside him was another servant, a silent, burly fellow with a thick neck and arms. He did not speak to Hannah. He wiped his mouth with his sleeve. Then he jammed his hands into his pockets and hurried on his way.

"Not very friendly, is he?" Hannah said. "Such foul weather makes everyone cross."

"Not me," Zach replied. He jingled as he twirled and pranced like the monkey from the street in London. "See how merry I am?"

Hannah laughed. She felt better already. "Don't let Reverend Phillips catch you. Saints don't dance."

"But Strangers do," Zach said and winked.

My Record of Remarkables

April 13, 1630

I vow not to spend any of my precious Time in Reading Romances or idle Poems, which tend only to raise false Ideas and impure images in my mind and leave a vile Tincture upon it. Are not these rats aboard ship the representations of our own evil thoughts?

When the fog lifts, another of God's providences. The

way is clear that we thought was cloudy. I decide I must fast these next days, though I tell no one. Dear Father says I am already too thin.

An idle, malicious servant gives me back my best silver thimble, but demands a kiss in return. I refuse. Later I review my actions and think perhaps I should have responded with more outrage. What is wrong with me?

Is it not true that I have never done any unworthy thing but acted most honorably and righteously as becomes a good Christian? When I was six years old, I was told that Hell awaited me if I did not repent. When I was seven, I learned to weep and look for signs of grace. When I turned eleven, I thought I had more grace than anyone else in the village. But now my moods swing between hope and despair.

I wonder if I am truly saved. This doubt terrifies me.

Chapter 7

*My dear Friend and Brother Caleb
at Chelmsford, who I always remember
with my best affection:*

Nearly three weeks at sea and a swallow
lighted on our ship! I know not where it
came from for we are so far from any land.
It was a pretty little bird that reminded me
of home. Once it rested, it flew away.
Where? I wish I knew. If only I could have
attached this letter to its sweet foot and sent
it back to you. Our first big storm two
weeks ago. The stiff gale tore a sail to
pieces. Enormous waves washed a tub of

fish that was to be our dinner overboard.
No one hurt, except the ship's cat, who was
drowned. Poor thing! Without a cat there is
no way to rid the ship of cunning, fearless
rats. Boys chase them for sport. The rats,
some say, have eaten heavily into our supply
of biscuits; others claim we have a thief
without a tail or whiskers on board.
Throughout the storm Abigail kept my spirit
up with riddles. When the sky finally
cleared, a sailor told me that the storm was
just a taste of what's to come. Our captain
complains that some passengers are nasty
and slovenly and that the gun deck where
the Saints are lodged is so beastly and noi-
some with victuals and other food that he
fears the danger of the health of the ship.
Now we have four people who must clean
for three days and then another four do the
job. Goody Garrett is worse. So weak she
can barely stand alone. We pray for her.
Father is so worried he will not leave her
side. I am glad I have Abigail for comfort.
One day I pray that you will join us in

America. When you do, be sure to bring plenty of warm clothes, for it is damp and cold aboard ship. Nothing ever dries. Our only heat is from small smoky cooking fires. Bring cheese and potted meat and sweets and other good things to eat because shipboard food meals are soon tiresome—salt pork Monday, salt beef Tuesday, dried peas Wednesday, salt pork Thursday, dried peas Friday, salt beef Saturday, and salt pork Sunday. Time will suffer me to write no more. Fare you well.

> Yours,
>
> Hannah aboard the *Arbella*
>
> April 29, 1630

One evening in early May Hannah could not sleep. The ship tossed and plummeted. Over and over, she heard the creak of timbers and the wash of waves against the ship. Somewhere above deck came the plaintive song of a fiddle. "Are you sick?" Abigail whispered.

"No," Hannah replied. She crept off of her

pallet, careful not to wake Goody Garrett, who had finally dozed off.

Abigail yawned sleepily. "Where are you going?"

"Up the hatchway for a gulp of fresh air."

"All right," Abigail said. She turned over and resumed snoring.

Hannah wrapped her cloak around herself and slipped on her shoes. She carried no lit candle. Even so, her feet found their way—just as Zach said they would. She quickly climbed up the ladder into the brisk air of the clear night. The black domed sky blazed with stars—a million trillion tightly packed, dazzling pinpricks of light. She had never seen so many stars before. The sight made her feel small and dizzy and awestruck. At that moment she recalled what Caleb had said. *All a marvelous display of infinite goodness.*

The sound of the wailing fiddle grew louder. The deck thumped now with rhythmic stomps. Three sailors jumped and danced to the merriment of the small gathering of other crew members. Hannah tapped her foot. She would have liked to have learned the hornpipe dance, too, but Father would never approve. The quarterdeck cabins blazed with light. She could hear laughter and the sound of voices and the clinking of tankards. The captain had invited guests from the *Jewel*. What were they eating? Hannah licked her lips, imagining roast duck with delicate, crispy skin and a thick black pudding. What she would not give to have even a crumb of Grandmother's gingerbread!

Somewhere she recognized a sound. Someone chewing. Was it a rat? She shrank back. "Hello?" she said softly. "Who goes there?"

"Saucy Zach."

Hannah laughed. "What are you eating?"

"Biscuit. Want one?"

Hannah could just barely make out the outline of Zach seated on the top of a barrel. "I'm tired of stale, dry biscuits," she said and climbed up on to another barrel. "An apple. I would give anything for a juicy apple."

"Then an apple it is," Zach said. He leaped from his barrel.

"Where are you going?" Hannah asked.

"To get you an apple." Zach vanished.

Another one of his exaggerations! Hannah impatiently hummed as she waited. There were no apples on board the ship. Not for passengers like her and her family. Zach was cruel to tease her like this.

"Here you are," Zach said, startling her.

Hannah held out her hand, expecting to be given a dusty, hard biscuit. To her amazement, she felt the small, cool, round shape of a small apple in her hand! She smelled it. The fresh aroma filled her nose with memories of Father's orchard. Delightedly she took a bite. The thin apple skin burst and filled her mouth with sweet, crunchy goodness. "Where?" she asked, chewing eagerly. "Where did you get this?"

"I have my sources," Zach replied mysteriously. "Is it good?"

Hannah could not speak, she was so busy nibbling away. "Delicious!" she said, licking sticky juice from her fingers. She wished she could admire the apple's bright color, its dappled, shining skin. But all was hidden by darkness. She ate every last bit, everything except the seeds and stem. Then she glanced contentedly up at the stars, swinging her feet back and forth so that her heels hit the barrel with a *thud-thud-a-thud.*

"Quiet!" Zach whispered.

Hannah stopped kicking. "Why do you care if I make that noise?" Suddenly she had a terrible thought. "Did you steal that apple, Zach?"

"No, I borrowed it."

In the darkness she could not see his face. She could only imagine his mocking expression. "Stealing is a sin," she said, filled with dread.

"And so is dancing around a Maypole. And cooking on Sabbath. And playing cards. And singing bawdy ballads and —"

"Stealing is serious, Zach. Stealing is worse." Hannah bit her lip. She could feel a piece of apple in her throat, caught there, almost choking her. *Am I a sinner, too?*

Zach laughed. "You are a great worrier. How many apples does Lady Arbella need?"

"Lady Arbella's apple?" Hannah squeaked, feeling even worse.

"Do you know what little food servants are

fed on this ship?" Zach asked in a low, angry voice. "Half rations of what you get. Half. Imagine that. And do you know what is served on Sir Saltonstall's table? Do you know what his daughters leave on their trenchers at their evening meals? Enough to feed two or three of us. What difference does a biscuit here or an apple there matter?"

Hannah crossed her arms in front of herself and held her elbows. *You are every moment in God's hands. His eye is always upon you.*

"How now, Moody?" Zach asked Hannah in a playful voice.

Hannah thought of the men walking the deck with their hands tied. She thought of the heads on pikes in London and the convicts chained along the Thames. "What will happen if someone finds out?"

"No one will find out," Zach said with great confidence. "I trust you with my secret."

Hannah wanted to feel pleased, but somehow she couldn't. Her shoulders slumped forward with the burden of what Zach had revealed. "I won't tell anyone," she said slowly.

Wind hummed through the rigging. Now the sailors played a sad, homesick song. The music floated out across the water up into the fathomless sky.

Zach cleared his throat and said,

> *"Where should this music be? In the air or the*
>   *earth?*
> *It sounds no more; and sure it waits upon*
> *Some god of the island. Sitting on a bank,*
> *Weeping again the king my father's wreck*
> *This music crept by me upon the waters*
> *Allaying both their fury and my passion*
>   *with its sweet air. . . ."*

"That's lovely," Hannah said. *In the air or the earth.* She liked the sound of the words. "Did you write that?"

Zach laughed. "I can't write. Can't read, either. I just memorized what I heard."

"Where?"

"In London at the theater. It's Shakespeare's play, *The Tempest.*"

"You have been to a real play?" Hannah

whispered. Father railed against the theater. *Rogues, pickpockets, and other unsavory types go there*, he said. *Theater's sinful, profane. Especially Shakespeare. Men dressed up like animals, cavorting like fairies and other cunning folk.* "What was it like in the theater?" she whispered eagerly. She had never met anyone who had actually been to a play.

"And, oh, what marvels!" Zach said. "It cost a penny to stand in the pit, the area around the stage where the music's very loud. That's where I go, up front so I can see. There's torches, candles, too, for light at night. I don't know how they do it, but the actors can make you see suns and moons and dragons with their words. There's duels and death scenes and ghosts and witches who come out of nowhere in a puff of smoke. Everyone in the pit and up in the gallery roars and cheers. Would you like to hear another speech?"

"Yes," Hannah said in a little voice. *Is it a sin to listen even if you're not at the theater?*

"Full fathom five thy father lies," Zach said in a mysterious voice that gave Hannah a chill.

"Of his bones are coral made;
  Those are pearls that were his eye;
  Nothing of him that doth fade
  But suffer a sea-change
  Into something rich and strange."

"I would say very strange indeed," a voice announced.

The hair on the back of Hannah's neck suddenly stood on end. *Abigail!* "What . . . what are you doing awake?"

"Enjoying the night air, just like you," Abigail replied sweetly. Too sweetly.

Zach jumped off the barrel with a thump. "Master Pyncheon's probably going to wonder where I've gone. Good night, ladies." With that, he vanished.

Hannah lowered herself carefully off the barrel. "It's getting cold. I think I'll go back, too."

"An odd boy. A Stranger," Abigail said in an even tone. "I don't trust him, Hannah. Neither should you."

Hannah did not reply. Thankful for the darkness, she hastily brushed every speck and seed of apple from her cloak. She held tight to the thunderbolt in her pocket and scurried across the deck and down the ladder back to her bed.

At four o'clock the next day, in fair weather, a shout went up from one side of the ship. Hannah, who had avoided her sister as best she could all day, ran to look. She was amazed to see something gray and gleaming floating as big as a little island—just a stone's throw away.

"Whale!" someone shouted. "All hands!"

The water swirled around the edges of the whale's great gleaming back. At one end, where its tail must have been, the water churned dangerously black, back and forth, back and forth. Fearless. Enormous. Hannah held her breath. What would it take for such an enormous, curious beast to move its body slightly—just enough—to knock against the ship? What would happen then? Would they sink?

"Whale coming round!" came a cry from high in the rigging.

The whale suddenly submerged. The *Arbella*

rocked slightly. Someone screamed. Hannah waited. Where did the whale go? The waves parted and foamed. The whale's head, round and gleaming, not like any other animal Hannah had ever seen before, came up and dipped under again. And to her astonishment, noisy, gushing water surged straight up! Wind caught the spray and sent wet droplets into the passengers' amazed faces. Hannah and the others stood there dripping, perplexed. Some Saints hid their eyes. Some prayed. Some fled. Hannah could not move. She wanted to see the whale's eyes. What color were they?

Suddenly, a few yards away, the whale reappeared. Someone screamed. Hannah still could not tear herself away from the sight of this huge fishlike creature, even as it smacked the water with its tail, rose up, then dived straight down, disappearing deep, deep. Who knew where?

"It's a sign!" the Reverend Phillips announced in a trembling voice. He launched into a sermon about the story of Jonah, the man whose sin and disobedience caused God to send a terrible storm. "And to save the lives of the other passengers and sailors on the ship," the Reverend Phillips boomed, "Jonah, a marked man, was thrown overboard and swallowed by a great whale."

Hannah listened, mesmerized. *A marked man.* She was certain the Reverend Phillips was speaking directly to her. *Can he tell what I've done? Does he know I ate a stolen apple?*

"Truth loves the light and is most beautiful when most naked," the Reverend Phillips concluded, glancing in her direction. "Amen."

He knows.

"Are you feeling all right?" Abigail asked when the sermon ended. "You look very pale." Tenderly she placed her hand on Hannah's forehead.

"I'm fine," Hannah said and shrank away.

The next day there was another shout on deck. At first Hannah thought it might be a second whale. She felt almost too fearful to look. But Father came with her this time. And when they came above deck, she saw Peaches being dragged across the deck by four sailors. A crowd of Saints heckled him. He spat and snarled at them even as his hands were being tied to a bar and a basket of heavy stones were hung about his neck with a rope. His face looked redder than ever. "A turd in all your teeth!" he cursed.

"What is happening, Father?" Hannah asked, terrified.

"This fellow," Father said, "was discovered bargaining with a child to sell him a box worth three pennies for three biscuits a day all the voyage. He'd received about forty and had sold them and many more to servants. He must stand and serve this punishment for four hours."

"What child sold him the stolen biscuits?" Hannah asked.

"That one. He has been justly punished by his master, I see," Father said and pointed.

There was Zach. One side of his face was bruised. His eye was swollen. He sat on the deck with a sign around his neck that said "Incorrigible." When Zach saw Hannah and her father, he scowled at her in a menacing way.

Hannah sucked in her breath hard. *He thinks I told on him.*

Flushed and sweating, she broke away from Father's side and hurried down into the hold. "Oh, Abigail, Abigail!" she said, sobbing into her waiting sister's arms. She buried her face in her sister's shoulder.

"There, there," Abigail murmured.

My Record of Remarkables

May 9, 1630

I woke up early and went to Reverend Phillips, a great learned man, and told him of my disquiet. I told him I was afraid I should go to Hell and was not elected. He asked me what he should pray for, and I said that God would pardon my sin and give me a new heart. He answered my fears as well as he could and prayed with many tears on my part.

After that my spirit was much lifted.

I feel satisfied that I did the right thing.

The Bible says:

VOYAGE TO A FREE LAND 1630

"He that go down to the sea in ships, that do business in Great Waters, see the works of the Lord, and his wonders in the deep."

We experience the Providence of great whales and leaping fish! What wonders are these strange creatures?

Chapter 8

Dear Brother Caleb at Chelmsford:

I will write, although it will do no good. I have no one to ask but you. If only I could read your wise answer or hear your kind voice! My friend thinks I betrayed him. I did not. Now he will not speak to me, he will not look at me. What should I do? How is it possible that this crowded ship could be such a Horrible lonely place?

Your sister Hannah

May 9, 1630

The next morning dawn crept in with a few shreds of pinkish sky. The wind was light, the sea calm. Hannah stood on deck and looked out over the water. The *Ambrose,* the *Jewel,* and the *Talbot* were only small distant shapes on the horizon. Her eyes burned. She had had so little sleep. All night Goody Garrett had tossed and moaned loudly. At dawn Father woke Hannah from a fitful sleep to tell her to go to the captain's cabin and give him a message. Now she needed all her courage to walk up the steps to the quarterdeck and knock on the captain's door.

"Sir?" she called in a small, terrified voice. "It's an emergency, sir."

"Who's there?" came a groggy, angry voice.

"Hannah Garrett, sir. Daughter of Richard Garrett, shoemaker."

The door swung open. The captain peered down at her with his hair standing straight up in spikes on his head. "What do you want?"

"It's . . . it's my stepmother, sir. She's in a bad way. My father begs you to send for the midwife from the *Jewel.*"

Captain Milborne swore an oath. "My first

real sleep in weeks," he muttered, "ruined for this!"

"Please, sir. She may die, my father says. Can you help us?"

"All right. I'll see what I can do. The *Jewel* is far ahead. We'll have to catch up and signal her somehow. Go tell your father we'll try."

"Thank you kindly, sir."

The captain's cabin door slammed shut. Hannah breathed a great sigh of relief. Slowly she returned to the hatch to tell Father the news.

Distraught, Father barely heard her words. He sat on a bundle of clothing, his head in his hands. "What this means, the Lord only knows, which in his due time He will manifest," he said in a low, mournful voice.

Hannah rested her hand on his bent shoulder to comfort him. She had no fondness for her stern stepmother, but she felt sad for Father, who seemed so lost and bewildered by what was happening.

Two other women from the ship, Goody Josselyn and Goody Kent, hovered about the pallet where her stepmother lay. A candle stub had been lit nearby. Goody Garrett's eyes were hollow and rimmed with dark circles. "We'll have to wait for the midwife and hope for the best," whispered Goody Josselyn, whose gaunt face reminded Hannah of a starving dog she once found in the woods.

Plump Goody Kent made a clucking sound when she saw Hannah. "There's nothing for you to do here, child. Be on your way."

Goody Garrett howled in terrible pain. Hannah backed away and nearly knocked over Abigail, who was also lingering nearby.

"Let's go above deck," Abigail said nervously. Together they climbed above deck to watch for the midwife's arrival.

"Do you think . . . do you think she will live?" Hannah whispered.

Abigail shrugged. "Only God knows that."

In the distance the girls watched as the sailors shouted and lowered the topsails. A gun went off from the *Arbella*'s stern. It was a signal for the *Jewel*. On the quarterdeck she could see Captain Milborne staring through a telescope. "She's hauling up her sails and waiting for us!" he shouted below.

How long will it take for us to get close enough? Hannah watched anxiously as the *Arbella* crept closer. Suddenly from the waves emerged a great series of splashes.

"Look!" Abigail cried. "Flying fish!"

"Dolphins!" a sailor shouted.

The deck was suddenly crowded with other passengers, all looking out into the water at the furious diving and leaping of twenty or more playful gray and white gleaming creatures. "See how they follow us and cavort in the water?" Hannah said. She clapped her hands with delight. *What strange manner of creatures are these?*

Abigail, too, seemed delighted. "See how they smile?" she said eagerly. "They are surely more works of the Lord. They are His wonders in the deep."

Sure enough the great swimming fish would rise so high out of the water that it was possible to see their eyes and mouths, which were upturned in such a friendly manner that Hannah wished she could leap into the water and follow them. Their bodies bent in arcs, their top triangle of skin pointing skyward. They splashed and chased one another, swimming ahead of the ship, circling it with great ease. *Mocking us just like the Wild Man.*

A little boy stood nearby. He lifted himself up to the railing to look over the edge. "How do they fly?" he asked.

"They have wings," the other boy replied. "They have manes and ears and heads and chase each other just like stone horses in the park in London."

His friend gave him a hard shove. "You lie."

Hannah smiled. She wondered where Zach was. He would enjoy all the excitement. Then she recalled how angry he probably was with her still. Her smile disappeared. She missed Saucy Zach. She missed his fascinating stories, his dangerous and wonderful speeches, his observations about the workings of the world. *How lonesome I will be if he never talks to me again the rest of the voyage!*

A shout rose up from the other side of the

ship. Hannah and Abigail ran to the other side and saw one of the sailors handling a long pole with a sharp iron end. A long rope was attached to the other end.

"Fire away, your worship," the sailor said, handing the long pole to Sir Saltonstall. "But watch the harpoon. It's more deadly than it looks. Aim for the head of the porpoise."

Hannah looked down into the water and saw something dark and solitary swimming beside the boat. It wasn't playful or daring like the leaping dolphins.

"Stand back, ladies," Sir Saltonstall said to his daughters, who shrieked and jumped up and down in anticipation.

Hannah and her sister watched in horror as Sir Saltonstall let fly the harpoon. The rest of the porpoises, knowing no fear, swam close by as if in a race.

"Stop!" Hannah shouted.

Too late. The harpoon flew through the air and sliced into the nearest animal. Blood spurted. The rest of the porpoises veered away.

"Hoist it up! Hoist it up!" Sir Saltonstall

shouted to the sailors. "It's the biggest fish I've ever caught. Bigger than any trout back in England. What do you think, ladies?"

Grace and Rosamond clapped and cheered. They stepped out of the way as the sailors pulled the big dripping gray and white creature up on the deck. Hannah was careful to avoid the two girls. She could hardly bear to watch the porpoise roll and flip its tail frantically, its great dark eye rolling in its head. Another sailor used a large mallet and quickly put an end to the porpoise's life. It lay on the deck, dripping, gleaming. Abigail and some of the other children crept closer and tried to touch it.

"Do he bite?" a little dirty boy asked.

"No. It's dead, foolish brains," his sister replied.

"The skin feels soft and slippery, like wet leather," Abigail confided in Hannah. "It doesn't seem like a fish at all."

Hannah wondered how her sister could be so bold as to pet a dead porpoise. *What if the fish is really a mortal man? What if it's an evil spirit?*

The sailors dragged the great body, which was nearly as tall as Hannah. They hung the porpoise up by its tail and began to butcher it. "We call them sea hogs," one of the sailors told Sir Saltonstall. "Tastes like rusty bacon or hung beef. Liver's the best part—boiled and soused in plenty of vinegar."

"Good man!" Sir Saltonstall said. He beamed with pride at the great porpoise. "I wish the lords and ladies back home could see this fine catch. Harpooning is a marvelous delight for recreation."

The sailors used large knives and quickly cut the porpoise into thin strips to be fried in small charcoal fires lit inside boxes of sand. As the men worked, they sang the songs that the Reverend Phillips called Foolish and Filthy. But everyone was so delighted at last to have fresh meat that no one complained about the terrible songs.

"More dolphins!" a sailor cried from high in the rigging.

Hannah looked out to sea. She saw another group of flying fish diving and swooping in and out of the water, this time with the speed and eagerness of a pack of wild dogs chasing a rabbit. Where were they going? She watched sadly as the creatures sped and danced around the ship.

"Get a fresh harpoon!" Sir Saltonstall ordered.

"No, sir," a sailor replied, eyes squinting. " 'Tis bad luck to kill a dolphin. Porpoises signal the forerunner of a gale of wind. But dolphins betoken storms."

Hannah watched the dolphins cavort and leap and was glad that no one would try to kill them. Where was the storm? She scanned the horizon and could see no sign of threatening clouds. Closer, closer came the *Jewel*. Another shot and a shout rang out from the *Arbella*. "Send the midwife over by skiff!" a sailor bellowed.

Another sailor aboard the *Jewel* waved as if he'd understood. Hannah watched closely, hoping that the midwife would arrive quickly and know what to do.

"Here's something to eat," Abigail said. She handed Hannah a piece of porpoise meat that had been cooked on a stick over a fire. Hannah sniffed the meat. The skin was blackened and smelled of bacon. Somehow she did not feel hungry anymore. She kept thinking of the friendly fish. *Poor thing!*

"Porpoise is very good. Better than salt pork, that's for certain," Abigail said. She nibbled a small piece. When she noticed that Hannah was not eating, she frowned. "What's the matter?"

"I don't want any," Hannah replied.

"Why?" Abigail asked crossly. "It may be weeks before we have fresh meat again."

"Then you eat my share."

Abigail scowled. "Perhaps a servant would like your portion. They are fed so little. Half rations. Imagine that."

Hannah suddenly sucked in her breath. *Imagine that.* Those were Zach's words. Hannah watched her sister chewing. Her fists curled tight. "You were hiding in the dark and listening to us talking. You're the one who told Zach's master and got him punished."

Abigail licked each finger with an annoying smack. "I warned you he wasn't to be trusted.

That boy is a scoundrel. He's incorrigible. He's a Stranger. He's a thief. I am just looking out for your best interests."

Hannah leaped to her feet and threw her meat down on the deck with such fury, the piece hit the boards with a loud *thud!* She tried to think of the very worst thing she could say to her sister. "Turd in all your teeth!" she said and stomped away.

She had to find Zach and tell him the truth. She felt so angry, so absorbed in her hatred for her sister, she did not hear the sailors talking as she passed. "Wind's shifting," one said, holding a finger aloft. "A backing wind."

"Aye, an ill wind," the other replied.

She did not see the midwife climb aboard from the small skiff belonging to the *Jewel*. She did not see the clouds massing on the horizon, big and black.

It took her quite some time to finally discover Zach. His face was still greenish yellow near his cheek. He sat in a dank corner belowdeck blacking Master Pyncheon's boots. His hands were filthy to the elbows, and he had a streak of grease on his nose that almost matched the color of the bruise on his forehead.

"Zach?" Hannah called in a small voice.

Zach did not look up.

"Zach?"

"What do you want?" He looked at her with a powerful hatred.

"You may not believe me, but I am telling you the truth," she said, taking a deep breath. "I wasn't the one who told your master about the stolen biscuits."

"I trusted you," he said and sneered.

"It wasn't me. It was my sister who told. She was hiding in the darkness, listening to us talking. She admitted it to me just now."

Zach resumed his polishing. "How do I know you tell the truth?"

Hannah thought for a few moments. She reached inside her pocket and found the thunderbolt. No one had ever seen it before. Not Abigail. Not Father. No one knew she had brought it all the way from England. She touched the tapered tip with her finger. "If I'm lying, you can keep this," she said slowly.

She held out the rock for him to examine.

Zach turned the thunderbolt over and over in his hand. "Fine stone. Looks like a dagger. Who gave it to you?"

"My brother."

Zach was silent for several minutes. He held the rock up to examine it. Then he pocketed it. Hannah gulped. Her pocket felt strange without the thunderbolt's heavy presence. What if her luck was gone now, too?

"If you're lying," Zach said slowly, "I'll soon know."

My Record of Remarkables

May 10, 1630

I read the Bible to my stepmother and try my best to be of some comfort. She has a fever, which makes her speak strangely in her sleep. She calls Caleb, Caleb, Caleb. When Dear Father hears this, he seems distraught.

Does she not know we already have one brother by that name? Hannah asks.

Dear Father does not reply. Instead he prays aloud

for God's goodness to deliver our stepmother from her trials and to help her see the error of her ways.

I begin to understand something that Hannah cannot. Something so terrible, I can tell no one. If God grants that this baby lives, he will not be our half-brother, he will be our nephew.

Chapter

9

Dearest Brother Caleb at Chelmsford:

Our stepmother bids I write to beg your
forgiveness and to thank you for your many
kindnesses to her. She asks that you pray on
her behalf. She suffers much and has given
up hope that she will live even though the
midwife has arrived. A greasy old woman
who delivered a baby on the *Jewel.* She has a
husky voice and tells us all the news. A
sailor died on her ship. A most profane,
proud fellow she called him, one very injuri-
ous to passengers. She says two servants
died of the cough on the *Ambrose.* I try to be

helpful to her. I run and fetch. Father can only pray. I think I will never marry—

❧

Hannah stopped writing. She lifted her pen from the paper that rested atop a trunk in the hold. The candle stub flickered. There. She heard it again. Shouts and the thud of footsteps from the deck above. Her ink bottle slid across the top of the trunk as the ship heaved. What was happening?

Another groan came from Goody Garrett's pallet. Goody Mason, the midwife, dozed nearby. She woke fitfully and scratched her neck, then fell to sleep again. In her lap she held her knitting. Close at hand she kept her bag with remedies such as camphor and herbs and a flagon of strong drink that she seemed to think nobody noticed when she took a quick sip every now and again.

When Hannah heard the light rapid footsteps she knew so well, she tucked the letter inside the trunk for safekeeping. "What took you so long?" Hannah asked her sister, who was carrying a basin of fresh water. "Did he talk to you?"

"Who?" Abigail asked. She placed the basin on the floor near Goody Garrett's pallet. Every so often the water sloshed to one side.

Hannah frowned. "You know who I mean. Zach. Did he ask to hear the truth?"

"Keep your voice down. Do you want the whole world to know?" Abigail hissed. "Yes, I spoke to him. I told him to fear God and pray for his salvation."

Hannah sighed loudly. "Did you tell him that you were the one who told his master about the stolen food?"

"I never had a chance. Not with all the insults he hurled in my direction. He said for me to keep my advice to myself and mind my own business. He loves a Saint, he says, as a dog loves a pitchfork."

Suddenly the floor shifted dizzily. The basin water spilled. The midwife's bag skidded across the floor. The candle burned blue and then sputtered out.

"What?" Goody Mason cried. "Where's me equipment?"

Someone shrieked. The ship lurched in the opposite direction. Trunks groaned and slid. Barrels and tools rolled as if in a landslide. The ship bucked and dived, sending Hannah flying. She groped in the darkness and struggled to her feet again, unhurt.

"Daughters of mine!" Father's voice rang out. "Where are you?"

"Over here!" Abigail called. "We can't find the candle."

"Have we hit an iceberg?" Hannah asked fearfully. "Are we sinking?"

"Bring a light this way, will you, sir?" Goody Mason said.

Father relit a candle and held it aloft. Silently he inspected their stepmother, who thrashed about in the bed. "How is she?"

"No better," Goody Mason said. She shook her head and fished up her bag of remedies. "The baby's small but breach. There's not much I can do."

"We must place our faith in God," Father announced.

"Father?" Hannah begged. She pulled on his

sleeve. "What is happening? Have the ships crashed together? Tell us."

"Do not worry. There has been no accident," Father said in a soothing voice. "A ship on a stormy sea is like a cradle rocked by a careful mother's hand. Though it moves up and down, it does not fall. A ship may often be rocked upon the troublesome sea. It does not sink or overturn, because it is kept by that careful hand of Providence by which it is rocked."

The ship lunged, then rolled. Hannah pitched against her sister. She did not feel the least convinced by Father's calm words. She wanted to see for herself what was happening and escape the choking darkness and foul air below. "Father, may I go above deck?"

"Why?" he demanded. "Goody Mason may need you here."

"The basin spilled. There's no fresh water," Hannah replied quickly. "I'll go get more." Before Father could refuse her request, she grabbed the basin, scrambled up the ladder, and pushed open the hatch.

Howling wind blew spray into her face. The

rigging sang. Canvas snapped and flapped. The rolling sea, patched now with white streaks, had turned the color of rotten meat. Overhead, big stormy petrels appeared. Hannah had not seen birds in weeks, and suddenly there they were. Where had they come from? The large white sea birds ominously circled the ships. *Is this some sign?*

"Looks like it's going to be wicked," a sailor said, rushing past. He and the rest of the crew scurried about with the same urgency that she had noticed the day they thought they were about to meet up with pirates. Sailors hauled down the sails. Others secured water barrels on deck with extra lengths of rope.

"Check the bilge pumps!" someone shouted. "Tell the passengers to double lash their belongings. She's a-coming on, boys. She's coming on strong."

Hannah struggled to keep her balance. She bent forward to walk across the deck. Lightning flashed. Anxiously she scanned a fleeing group of passengers for a sign of Zach.

"Get below!" Peaches shouted over the roar of wind and waves.

"Where's Zach?" she said as loudly as she could.

"I don't know. Get below and save your own hide."

The ship lurched. A group of terrified passengers struggled down the hatchway, trying their best not to plunge forward down the ladder. As they descended, she caught sight of a broad-brimmed hat.

"Zach!" she called.

He moved down the hatchway, as if he had not heard her.

"Zach!"

He turned, flashed a glance in her direction, and climbed down even faster. "Stop!" She ran to him and grabbed his arm. "My sister didn't tell you, did she?"

"What?" He held one hand to his unbruised ear. He scowled. "Get below. Storm's blowing."

Hannah tucked the basin under her arm and followed him into the hold. Water dripped down her neck. She felt wet and cold to the bone. "Why didn't you speak to my sister and ask her to tell you the truth?" she demanded.

Zach said nothing for several moments. He coughed and finally answered, "I don't like to talk to her."

"Zachariah PUNT!" a shout rang out.

"It's the old mule, mad as ever. Curse him," Zach murmured. "I must go."

Hannah sighed with disappointment. At that moment she felt as empty as the basin in her hands.

My Record of Remarkables

May 10, 1630

What new tests are these that God has made for us to endure? A vicious sailor seeks to torment my family by dropping a dead rat into the drinking water I'm carrying. Our stepmother's suffering begins in earnest. I tell her when she feels these pains, to think of martyrdom and Hell. She throws a shoe at me and accuses me of wishing her dead.

Dear Father struggles to give her comfort but cannot.

My sister accuses me of using her ill. I must take better care of her as my own Tender Mother took care of me. Hannah can not understand how I tried to help her. Maybe someday she will. Let there be something of benevolence in all that I speak to her from this day forward.

I resolve never to allow the least measure of any fretting or uneasiness to disturb my Dear Father. I resolve to refrain from an air of dislike, fretfulness, and anger in conversation, but to exhibit an air of love, cheerfulness, and benignity.

Sir Saltonstall's daughters display their lovely lace fans and brilliant green velvet gloves while laughing and whispering tittle-tattle and silliness. Were I to have such lovely clothes! God forgive me.

The way to grow in any grace is the exercise of that grace. I tried my best to make myself known to the impertinent servant. He refuses to listen. His soul may be damned forever. It pains me to think of his beautiful eyes.

A very strong wind. The billows run as high as mountains; yes, as mountains. They are extremely large and majestic, and exhibit the great power of their creator, as pleasing as they are fearful to behold. I wish that I could speak to Kitty. All around me is nothing but confusion and sadness. There is no one to whom I can unburden my heart. . . .

Throughout the day and into the night the storm pounded the ship. Without even a lantern or a cooking fire, there was nothing to see, nothing hot to eat. Hannah and Abigail sat wedged against one of the securely fastened barrels for protection. Every so often as the ship lurched and dropped, another chest or kettle or box broke free and crashed through the dark hold, battering and bruising anyone in its way. Some passengers prayed. Some wept. Some shouted in rage and frustration.

"Will the storm never end, Father?" Abigail asked.

"Only God knows that," Father replied slowly.

"'The Lord bowed the heavens and came down, thick darkness under his feet. The channels of the dark were seen and the foundations of the world were laid bare!'" shouted the Reverend Phillips. "The raging sea expresses God's power and glory. This storm is provoked by combat with the Devil."

Hannah did not find either Father's or the pastor's words comforting. She reached inside her empty pocket. The thunderbolt! Zach had never given it back. What if he'd lost it? What if it was gone forever? Hannah slumped against her sister.

"You are tired. Why not sleep?" Abigail said. "Lean on my back."

Hannah closed her eyes. But she could not sleep. The ship bucked and heaved. "What's that around my legs?"

"Water," Abigail said in a trembling voice. "Father? Father!"

Goody Josselyn shrieked, "A leak!"

"We'll all drown!"

"My God, we're going to die. All of us."

A candle flared. And in the half-light Hannah could see the horrible truth. Water seeped between two boards in the hull. The Reverend Phillips took off his coat and stuffed it against the crack. "Someone tell the captain!" he cried. "In the meantime, let us do what we can. 'And I saw as it were a sea of glass mingled with fire. . .'"

"What prayers are to be made in such perils at sea?" Goody Mason grumbled.

Cold water sloshed ankle-deep across the

floor. Hannah watched Father trying as best he could to lift Goody Garrett to a safe, dry space atop three chests pushed together. Goody Mason snagged her bag before it floated out of reach. To escape from the water, Hannah climbed up the hatchway ladder. In the darkness all around her, she could hear only cries for help. She had to get out. She looked up. She had to climb on deck and tell the captain about the leak. As quickly as she could, she scrambled the rest of the way up the ladder. She pounded furiously on the hatchway overhead. "Let me out! Let me out!"

No answer.

She pressed her ear against the hatchway. But the pounding of the waves and wind were all that she could hear. She shoved as hard as she could. "We've sprung a leak!" she screamed. "We're going to drown!"

"Let me help," Zach said. He hurried up the ladder. Together they pushed with all their might. The hatchway opened a crack. Icy wind and rain blew into their faces. Hannah pushed harder, raising the hatch little by little with help from Zach.

She peered out and could see only sailors' boots rushing past. Waves washed over the deck. She had to find the captain. "Come on!" Zach cried. He pushed the hatchway open, and she crept out on to the deck, clinging to the nearest thing she could lay her hands on to steady her balance. She stood and watched out the corner of her eye as Zach climbed out on to the deck as well.

"We're leaking below!" she shouted to a sailor hurrying past. But he paid no attention to her.

Wind shrieked in the rigging. Ragged spray and rain drove sideways, thick and hard. She could no longer make out the lantern that hung in the poop deck. It was only a white blur. Zach had disappeared. She could barely see her hand in front of her face. When the rain lessened for a moment, she was able to glance over one shoulder, out to sea. The sight made her suck in her breath hard. A black mountain rolled toward the ship, taller than the highest tip of the mast. She could feel the deck below her feet begin to shift as one end of the ship rose crazily upward to meet the wall of water. She fell to her knees and clung to the deck as best she could. At that moment she thought of Chelmsford and how once long, long ago she had climbed to the top of a snowy hill, brilliant with sunlight, and heard her brother calling to her, "Dumpling? Dumpling!"

"Hold on!" someone shouted.

Then the cold shrill darkness slammed against her like a fist.

Chapter

10

Hannah tumbled head over heels. Blinding, icy water swallowed her. She held her breath and tried to move her bruised arms to catch hold of something—anything. Her hands scraped against objects rough and wrist-thick. Rope! She grabbed but felt herself sinking deeper. She kicked. Her long skirt tangled around her ankles and feet. Rope snared her legs. Something bulky bumped and scraped heavily against her face. She clung, then tried clawing her way up toward what she hoped was the surface. More rope yanked past, burning her hands, her cheeks.

Air! She must get air! Deeper, blacker darkness edged in on all sides as if she were falling into a bottomless well. *How can this be happening?* She struggled to move, to free herself. *I can't drown. Not now. I never got the thunderbolt back from Zach. I never said goodbye to Caleb.* Father's skull-like face floated past. *"Of his bones are coral made. Those are pearls that were his eye."* Father frowned and shook his head at her as if she were a great disappointment. Hannah felt embarrassed. *"Why did you disobey and go on deck?"* his voice rang in her ears. *"What a senseless way to die."*

Hannah's throat burned. She felt as if a great vise were being screwed against her chest, pressing her lungs against her spine. Tighter, tighter. How long till she burst? Now Zach's face floated past. He laughed and mocked her. *"This ship's got enough skeins, coils, and tangles to remind a person of the gallows. I suppose that is a comfort if you prefer hanging to drowning."*

Drowning! She didn't want to drown. *What if I'm swallowed by a whale? What if I go to Hell?* She grappled with the rope and pulled herself up.

Up. Up. Gulping bubbles passed before her face. No matter how hard she tried, she could not reach the surface. She paused, exhausted. Her dress floated past her waist. *How painless and easy a death by drowning might be. Like falling about in a green field in early summer.* She gulped less and less for air. But the pressure on her chest only became more unbearable.

Late spring in Grandmother's garden. Everything blooming and fragrant in warm sunlight. Frogs croak. Bees buzz. There is Caleb. He smiles and sings to me in his sweetest voice: "When daffodils begin to peer, With hey! The doxy o'er the dale . . ."

Gradually the pain in her chest eased. She saw the broad flat fields outside Chelmsford. Grain swept by the wind moved like pale waves back and forth, back and forth. Overhead, clouds raced and the sky glinted bright and blue. And she felt a sad longing to see her sister again. *If we could only go home to Chelmsford where it is warm and safe and . . .*

Suddenly her arms were wrenched upward. Something burned her scalp. Even as she was yanked out of the raging waves, she tried to keep her eyes shut. She did not want to wake up. She wanted to keep thinking of peaceful Chelmsford, but she couldn't.

"Open your eyes, girl!" someone screamed in her face. "Breathe, damn you!"

She blinked. Light blinded her. Wind roared. *What is happening?* Something hard and sharp stung her face. *Where am I?* She pitched forward and vomited. She felt as if all her insides were coming out. She vomited more bitter seawater, gallons and gallons. She paused. And when she thought she had nothing left inside, she vomited again.

"That's good!"

Dripping and miserable, she struggled to sit up. Someone pounded her on the back. She coughed.

"She'll be all right. She's a sturdy thing."

The deck lurched. Lightning flashed. Thunder rolled. A terrific cracking noise filled the air. She could feel herself sliding. With all her might, she dug her fingers and nails into the wood. She would not go back. *Not to that dark, cold place again.*

"The main mast!"

Bleary-eyed, Hannah glanced up in time to see a great flame settle upon the tallest upright wooden post that ordinarily held the ship's biggest sail. Now the sail was gone and only the skeletal remains of the mast itself pointed skyward, like a dead man's finger. The strange fire danced up and down, then vanished. *What wondrous thing is this?* Hannah rubbed her eyes. *Am I dead and in heaven?*

"Take her below!"

Someone who looked very much like Peaches lifted her roughly and carried her below. She shivered uncontrollably. "Where is Zach?" she demanded. "What happened to Zach?"

"Don't say nothing. Just sleep," Peaches said. He descended the ladder and set her down in the dark hold on something soft. "What you need now is rest."

But Hannah did not want to rest. She wanted to find Zach. *Was he washed overboard, too?* Nearby, she heard someone crying. A sad sobbing and keening as if a person's heart would break. "Abigail?" Hannah whispered hoarsely. "Abigail?"

Her sister bent over her, clutching her hand so tightly it hurt. "Is it you? Is it really you?"

"Miss, give her some blanket. She's shaking like a dog in January," Peaches said. "I'll see to getting those bilge pumps to work." His heavy footsteps clomped across the hold and disappeared in a slow, weary shuffle.

"Now, now. Be a good girl and drink this," a husky voice said. Goody Mason held something hot next to Hannah's face. It was a cup of tea laced with something strong.

"Is she all right?" Father asked anxiously. His face hovered nearby, filled with concern. "Her lips are bluish. Why does she shake like that?"

"Out of my way so I can do my job, sir," Goody Mason ordered. Hannah felt the warmth of the tea going down her sore throat. Goody Mason removed her dripping dress and replaced it with something warm and dry. She tucked extra blankets around her feet and shoulders.

In the welcome warmth Hannah's eyelids grew heavy. More than anything, she wanted to sleep. But there was the crying again. The terrible weeping. Suddenly she remembered. Her eyes opened wide. "Abigail?" she whispered. "Did Goody Garrett die?"

"No," Abigail said and sniffed.

"The baby?"

"Not born yet."

"Then why are you crying?"

Abigail snuffled loudly again. "I thought you drowned. I thought you were gone from us forever."

Hannah struggled to remove her arm from the blanket so that she could reach out and pat grieving Abigail. But she did not have the strength. "There, there," she said instead, using the tender voice of the big sister who always knew what to do. "There, there . . . "

And then she drifted off to sleep.

In her dream the storm continued to rage and blow. There were nights of wind and rain. The mountainous sea was so very wide and the boat so very small. So very small. Floating like a cork. The sailors rushed about on deck. The masts flamed.

Suddenly Peaches shouted and pointed. When she looked out among the great black waves, she saw Zach swimming. He popped his head up above the water and smiled at her. She called to him. Peaches and the other sailors threw out a triple line of very stout nets. But Zach only laughed and swam farther away. Over and over he came up from the deep water and gazed at Hannah and the sailors. Then he dived down and vanished. "He's escaped," Peaches called. "He's never coming back. . . . "

When Hannah woke up, images from the terrible dream continued to dance through her head. *An evil spirit lurking in the body of a drowned man.* Hannah shook so hard, her teeth chattered. *A fish pretending to be a human being.*

"The Lord showed his dreadful power toward us and yet his unspeakable rich mercy," Father said, his voice sounding very far away. "Amen."

Hannah blinked hard, hoping she was awake and safe in the hold with her family. She heard the muted roar of the waves through the hull. The ship rocked and pitched, but less violently than before.

"Feeling better?" Goody Mason asked. She placed a damp cloth on Hannah's forehead.

Hannah nodded. Nearby she could see the slumped, sleeping form of Abigail. In her lap was a piece of embroidery. "Abigail?" she whispered desperately. "Abigail?"

Her sister opened her eyes and yawned. "What?"

"Is Zach drowned?"

"No one knows. No one's been above deck. His fate is in God's hands."

Hannah turned away from her sister. She pulled the blanket up over her shoulder and head so that no one could see her cry. At least Abigail had not called Zach a most profane, proud fellow who deserved to die. At least she could be glad of that.

In the extremity and appearance of Death, as distress and distraction would suffer us, we cried unto the Lord, and he was pleased to have compassion and Pity upon us. For by his overruling providence and his own immediate good hand, he guided the shipmen to save my sister's life and brought her back to me ALIVE.

For this I will be forever grateful. Thanks be to God . . .

Chapter

11

Dear Brother Caleb at Chelmsford,

My most kind remembrance to you and
Grandmother whom in this world I never
looke to see againe. But ye will of God be
done. Our voyage hither hath been as full of
crosses as ourselves have been of crooked-
ness. I feel obliged to put pen to paper to tell
you the Sad news. On Sunday last our stepmother was delivered of a Child still borne.
She had some mischance which caused her
to come neere a month before her time. The
babe was the second death and burial at sea
of the voyage. How it saddens me to think

the poor thing was never baptized! God's will be done.

We have journeyed thru many sore and terrible storms. I have never thought such weather to be possible. The wind blew mightily and the waves tossed us horribly. Waves poured themselves over the ship and caused a leak below. One storm was so fierce and the seas so high as the ship could not bear a knot of sail but was forced to drift under bare poles for divers days together. Our sister Hannah coming upon some occasion above the gratings on to the deck was with the roll of the ship thrown into the sea. But she caught hold of the topsail halyards, ropes that hung overboard and ran out at length. Yet she held her hold, though she was sundry fathoms underwater, till sailors hauled her up by the same rope to the brim of the water and then with a boathook and other means got into the ship again and saved her life. Thanks be to God. She was something ill with it. Her rescue the Reverend Phillips sees as a true sign of Providence.

Pray for us. The Lord make me strong in him & keepe both you and Grandmother.

> Your dutiful sister,
> Abigail aboard the *Arbella*
> May 22, 1630

❧

"How now, Moody?"

Hannah opened her eyes. To her astonishment, there stood Zach, smiling ear to ear. He wore a sailor's too-big blue jacket, leather breaches of gray frieze, and around his neck was loosely knotted a red scarf.

"Are you a ghost?" she muttered, trembling.

Zach laughed. "No, I am very real. When I helped Peaches with your rescue, I impressed Captain Milborne so much that he issued me these fine clothes. How do you like my outfit? Captain says if I work hard, some day I can be a topman."

Hannah was too stunned to speak. Slowly she sat up on the pallet and peered at Zach. "I'm grateful for your help in my rescue, but what's a topman?"

"The seaman who works aloft, high above the deck in the rigging and sails. It's dangerous work."

"What says your master?"

"Nothing."

"How can that be?" she demanded. *Why would Master Pyncheon allow his servant to suddenly become a sailor?*

"My master has no opinion about my new career."

Hannah rubbed her temples. Zach's senseless chatter was making her head throb. *Is he exaggerating again?* "Why has he no opinion?"

"He cannot speak," Zach said.

"What foolishness are you telling me? Your master is as full of wind as anyone I know."

"No more," Zach said in a mournful voice.

"No more?"

"My master cannot speak because he's 'full five fathoms deep.'"

"He's dead?"

Zach nodded solemnly. "Buried at sea a fortnight ago. His heart stopped of fright during the storm." A sly grin crept across Zach's face.

"I do not miss him, his mad jack moods or his beatings."

"I see," Hannah said, although she still felt confused. "What is the day?"

"The day?"

Hannah sighed. "How long have I been asleep?"

"A very long time, Lazy Bones. We've nearly reached the Grand Banks. And according to my reckoning, this is the fifty-eighth day of our voyage."

"The fifty-eighth day," Hannah murmured in wonderment.

Zach reached into the pocket of his coat. Sheepishly he handed Hannah the thunderbolt. "I'm returning this to you with thanks. Miss Prat-A-Pace told me everything."

"Miss Prat-A-Pace, is it?" Abigail demanded, suddenly appearing from the shadows. She thumped a bowl of porridge on the floor beside Hannah. "Better Miss Prat-A-Pace than Bite-Finger-Baby. Take your fingers out of your mouth, Hannah."

Hannah hid the thunderbolt in her pocket.

She picked up the spoon and rapidly ate the porridge, all the while studying her sister as if she were seeing her for the first time. She and Abigail had the same high forehead, the same embroidered coif. She knew her sister well enough to be able to guess most times what she was thinking without her saying a word. *How is it that we are so alike and yet so different?*

"Why are you smiling at me like that?" Abigail demanded. She put her fists on her hips. Then she turned to Zach. "You best be on your way, Stranger."

"Zach need not be sent away," Hannah said in a firm voice. "Not after he saved my life. Give me your hand, Zach, and pull me up. I'm afraid I've lost my sea legs."

Zach chuckled and did as he was told. Hannah handed her sister the empty bowl. "Where do you think you're going?" Abigail demanded.

"Above to get some air," Hannah replied. "You have a very lovely smile when you show it, Abigail. Will you come with us?"

Abigail blushed and shook her head. "No, I will stay here."

"Do as you please," Hannah said. She kissed her startled sister on the cheek.

Hannah and Zach tiptoed past the pale, sleeping figure of Goody Garrett. Her hair lay in tangled, stringy wisps about her pillow. Her face looked small, pinched. She did not look anything like the fierce, energetic woman Hannah had known back in Chelmsford. "Is she better?" Hannah whispered to Zach.

"I hear she's still weak and grieving," Zach replied. "Perhaps the tonic of free air in the New World will help. One whiff will cure anyone of what ails them." A shot rang out from above. Then another. Zach cocked his head to one side. "A signal to the other ships. They're sounding to see how deep the ocean is beneath us."

"Why?" Hannah asked anxiously.

Zach rolled his eyes as if she were nothing but a stupid landsman. "Every two hours the crew lowers a sounding lead coated with tallow at one end. This collects the sand and tells the captain how far away we are from shoals off the coast. Yesterday at eighty fathoms there was fine gray sand."

"Is that good?"

"Let me just say," Zach replied with authority, "that the shoals to the south off Nova Scotia are perilous enough that the captain fitted on a new main sail strong and double in case we must maneuver out of the way of danger. With a bit of luck, Peaches told me, we'll soon see land."

"Land!" Hannah exclaimed. With all her strength, she pulled herself up the ladder. Zach followed close behind.

Overhead Hannah heard the great skuas swooping over the water. The large seabirds cried *hah-hah-hah* in rasping voices. How wonderful to feel the fresh breeze against her face! The sky was clear. A small, handsome gale flapped the canvas and hummed in the rigging. The gentle sea rolled dull green gray, a dense color that swallowed light instead of reflecting it. *So different from the stormy scene I remember.* She searched the western horizon, but saw nothing that looked like land. She leaned on the side of the ship. "What will the New World look like?"

"Like nothing you have ever seen before," Zach said and licked his lips. "Sweet succulent fruits called persimmons grow in great ropes like onions. Huge turkeys run in flocks of hundreds. When the ducks fly overhead, there are so many that the air rushes and vibrates like a great storm coming through the trees. A hunter need only point his gun skyward and his dinner falls to the ground."

Hannah turned and lowered herself so that she sat in a pool of sunlight on the deck. She smiled, tilted her head back, and closed her eyes so that she might feel the warm, bright light against her eyelids. She tried to imagine what kind of perfect house Father would build, one big enough certainly for Caleb when he came across the ocean to join them. There would be a garden, too. And plenty of wild birds to visit and . . .

"What's that?" Zach announced.

Hannah opened her eyes. "What?"

"Down in the water. Do you see it?"

Hannah jumped to her feet to look into the rolling waves and was surprised to see a floating, fragile yellow shape.

"A butterfly!" Zach cried happily.

Hannah looked closely. "But it's dead. Poor thing!"

"Don't you see what this means? A butterfly cannot fly as far as a bird. Land must be nearby!"

All day Hannah and Zach kept watch for the first glimpse of the New World. But it wasn't until the afternoon of the next day, after a thick mist parted, that the first scudding dark, low shape was spotted on the horizon.

"Land ho!" a sailor cried high in the rigging.

Hannah rushed to the deck and looked to the west. She saw something that seemed more like cloud than land. By nightfall the wind calmed and mist returned. Nothing was visible again.

"Where is the land?" Hannah asked Father as he tucked her into her bed that evening. "What if we miss it altogether?"

"Do not fear, daughter of mine. Our captain is a wise, experienced seaman. He knows the way. Did you say your prayers?"

Hannah nodded.

"Go to sleep now," Father said and left her.

But Hannah could not sleep. "Do you suppose," she whispered to Abigail, "that the land we saw was only a dream?"

"What a stupid question!" Abigail replied. "Shut your eyes."

Hannah did not shut her eyes. She stared into the darkness, listening to the lullaby of waves sloshing against the hull and the gentle *creak creak creak* of the rigging. Something scratched and scampered in the darkness. But she had become so accustomed to the scurrying sounds, she did not flinch. *What will happen to the rats when we reach America?* She imagined a parade of furry creatures marching down the gangplank. *Of course, each one will carry his own small bag of belongings—a bit of cheese, a scrap of biscuit . . .*

"Do you suppose that after we arrive," Hannah whispered urgently to Abigail, "our English rats will get along with their American cousins?"

Abigail groaned. "Go to sleep, Hannah!"

The next day dawned clear and bright. By afternoon the sun shone so warm that Hannah slipped her cloak from her shoulders. "See, over there!" she said to Abigail, who stood beside her on deck, where a small crowd of children had gathered to enjoy the sunshine. The girls could see in the far distance what looked like small islands. "Smell that coming from the shore?" Hannah took a deep breath.

Abigail closed her eyes and sniffed, too. "Just like Grandmother's garden in summer."

"Green trees, that's what I miss," Hannah said dreamily. "Lots of leaves that make noises in the wind. Grass that bends and whispers."

"Flowers, plenty of flowers," Abigail said and opened her eyes. "Red roses and yellow marigolds and bright, fragrant purple phlox."

"A bee or two would be nice."

Abigail frowned. "Not too many."

"And don't forget frogs and snakes."

Abigail rolled her eyes. "How you vex me!"

Hannah grinned. She gave her sister's elbow a gentle squeeze. "What's that?" she said, pointing skyward. A bedraggled gray-brown shape fluttered, then landed in the rigging. She ran closer for a better look. "It's a pigeon!" But when she turned to look at her sister, she saw that

Abigail had a strange, sad expression on her face.

"It's not as fine as the pigeons back home," Abigail murmured.

"New England is an earthly paradise," Hannah said in a bright voice. "Just wait. You'll see."

Abigail gave half a smile, but she did not look convinced.

My Record of Remarkables

The sins of men are like the raging sea which would overwhelm us all. Master Pyncheon is buried at sea, sewn up in an old blanket with two or three cannon balls tied to his feet and then heaved overboard. Prayers and salutations accompanied his body into the bowels of the Great Atlantic. His servant becomes indentured to our captain and seems to exalt in his new position. I still do not trust him but find his new uniform hand-some.

I grieve for the other death. The small unchristened body in the deep! Dear Father, too, seems broken by the loss.

Our stepmother has suffered enough. May God forgive her. She allows me to comb her hair, which is long and tangled and full of mites. For once she has no hard words for me and seems pleased to be gently treated. Perhaps she may one day return the favor to me and my sister.

And what shall become of us in this new land? How strange that it is my sister now who soothes and placates my fears! I must have courage like Hannah's.

The Lord sent the terrible storm at sea to awaken me. The deliverance from that tempest is so sweet. I was pulled from an apparent Death and given a new life. Praise God!

Chapter 12

Dearest Brother Caleb at Chelmsford:

What good fortune! You will be delighted
to know that we have seen land for four
days now. Thick trees can be spotted very
plainly. We pass many rocky islands, some
with Small hills. We have a fine fresh smell
from shore that makes me anxious to run
and jump on solid ground again. Yesterday
we were within sight of Cape Anne, and
today our captain says that once we find a
place to anchor we will go ashore in our
small boats. The names here are so strange
and difficult to say—Pascataquay and

Nahumkeeke and Agawame. Smoke from Indians' fires can be seen. This makes Abigail fearful. She hears stories from some of the other girls and believes that she will be killed and her hair will be stolen by savages. I do not believe her hair is that beautiful. I must hastily close because our letters go aboard the *Mary and John*, a ship heading home. Come soon, dearest brother and friend. Pray for us as we pray for you.

> Hannah on the *Arbella*
> June 12, 1630

The next day Hannah sat restlessly beside her sister in a small boat rowed by two sailors and Zach. The heavily loaded craft was bound for Salem. Every so often Abigail turned and looked back toward the *Arbella*, where Father and Goody Garrett watched from the railing. Their turn would come next.

The rocky shore ahead was lined with tall, dark trees. The air smelled of pine and fragrant wood smoke. "With so much wood to burn, we'll be warm in winter," Hannah said to her sister in an encouraging voice. "Warmer even than the nobility back home."

Her sister frowned. "In the deepest darkest part of the forest, there may be many wild and ferocious beasts."

"Is that true?" Hannah asked Zach.

"For beasts," he replied, "there are bears and several sorts of deer. That's what some sailors told me. Also wolves, foxes, beavers, otters, martins, and wild cats, and a great beast called a moose—as big as an ox."

Hannah made an impressed whistling sound. "As big as that? You see, Abigail, there will be plenty to eat."

"And where are the houses? Where is the church?" Abigail peered at the clearing where a dozen twig huts stood huddled together. "I see no shops, no streets, no carriages or carts. The growing season is much advanced, yet there are no vast fields planted with wheat. How will we have bread? What will we eat when winter comes?"

Hannah, Abigail, and Zach studied the small, struggling settlement. Zach turned away from the girls and began rowing, slower now. Abigail brushed something away from her eyes.

"It will take some time. There is much work to be done," Hannah said quietly. "Father said we should not be discouraged."

Abigail sniffed. "I want to go back."

"To the *Arbella?*" Hannah whispered.

"No, to England."

"Don't be afraid." Hannah slipped from her pocket the thunderbolt. "Here's a bit of home to keep for luck and courage. Caleb gave me this thunderbolt before we left. He found it in a field after a storm. Do you see that pattern there? If you look very carefully, you can imagine the stars and galaxies over Essex."

Abigail turned the slender, tapered stone over and over in her hands. "You brought this all the way across the ocean?"

Hannah nodded. She glanced at Zach. "I had some help keeping it safe on the long journey. Now the thunderbolt belongs to you."

Abigail looked at her sister and then at the thunderbolt with a kind of wonderment. "Are you certain?"

Hannah nodded. "I don't need it anymore."

Abigail smiled. She held the thunderbolt in her cupped hand as if it were some precious, forgotten memory.

Zach nudged Hannah. "Do you see yonder?"

Hannah shielded her eyes from the sun. Along the beach she spied children from the *Arbella*. They waved and danced in happy circles, calling, "Strawberries! We found wild strawberries!"

"Hurry!" shouted Zach to the other oarsmen. Hannah slipped into the seat beside him. She took one oar. He took the other.

"Sing with us, Abigail," Hannah said.

And for once her sister did not hesitate to join in as they rowed all the way to shore, singing:

> *"Tell 'em all, tell 'em all,*
> *Gallowbirds all, gallowbirds all*
> *Great and small, great and small*
> *One and all, one and all."*

June 12, 1630

Not wishing any pain or suffering to be caused if this small book were to be discovered, I have decided to consign it to the fire. I do this in the spirit of complete forgiveness, resolving never to do anything which I would not be afraid to do, if it were my last hour of life.

Here endeth this endeavor to reveal the Heart of Abigail G.

Author's Note

This book is based on the true story of the *Arbella*, which left England and crossed the North Atlantic in 1630 as part of one of the largest migrations of Puritans seeking religious freedom and economic opportunity in the New World. Many of the passengers on the *Arbella* were families with children. Thanks to a journal kept by the future governor of the Massachusetts Colony, John Winthrop, we know many details about the hardships and difficulties, joys and discoveries experienced on the three-month journey.

The Garrett family was included on the list of

passengers aboard the *Arbella*. During a particularly hard winter of 1630–31, Winthrop tells us a few more details about what happened to the Garrett family after they landed. These are his exact words:

"December 25, 1630 —

But this day the windd came n:w: verye stronge & some snow withall but so Colde as some had their fingers frozen & in danger to be loste . . .

December 26 —

The rivers were frozen up, & they of Charleton could not come to the Sermon at Boston, till the afternoone at highe water. manye of our Cowes & goates were forced to be still abroad for want of houses. Rich. Garrard a shoemaker of Boston & one of the Congregation there, with one of his daughters a yonge mayde, & 4: others went towards Plimouthe in a Shalloppe, against the advise of his friends . . . the winde overblew so much at n:w as they were forced to come to a Killicke (throw out an anchor made of stone encased in a wooden frame) at 20 fathoms: but their boat drew & shaked out the stone, & they were putt to sea, & the boat tooke in muche water, which did freese so harde, as they could not free her: so they gave themselves for lost, & Commendinge themselves to God, they disposed themselves to dye, but one of their Companye espying lande, neere Cape Cod, they made shifte providence; were Carried through the rockes to the shore; where some got on lande, but some had their legges frozen into the Ice so they were forced to be cutt out: being come on shore they kindled a fire, but having no hatchet they could gett little wood, & were forced to lye in the open ayre all night, being extremely Colde . . ."

Thanks to the generosity of two Indian women, who discovered the shipwrecked group, help arrived. The Indians housed and fed several members of the group and tried valiantly to restore their boat so that they could return the survivors to Plymouth.

Unfortunately, Garrett died. He was buried

by the Indians, who heaped his grave with branches to keep away wolves. Of the entire party, three more died of exposure and severe frostbite before they reached their home. The one who survived with least injury was Garrett's daughter. As Winthrop wrote, "... the girle escaped beste...."

I like to think that girl was Hannah.

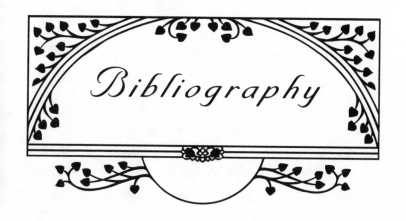

Bibliography

PRIMARY SOURCES

Ames, Azel, ed. *Mayflower and Her Log.* New York: Houghton Mifflin, 1901.

Dunn, Richard S., Savage, James and Yeandle, Laetitia, eds. *The Journal of John Winthrop, 1630–1649.* Cambridge: The Belknap Press of Harvard University Press, 1996.

Hanscom, Elizabeth Deering, ed. *The Heart of the Puritan: Selections from Letters and Journals.* New York: The MacMillan Company, 1917.

James, Sydney V., ed. *Three Visitors to Early*

Plymouth: Letters About the Pilgrim Settlement in New England During its First Seven Years. Plymouth, Mass. 1963.

BOOKS

Anderson, Virginia DeJohn. *New England's Generation: The Great Migration and the Formation of Society and Culture in the Seventeenth Century.* New York: Cambridge University Press, 1991.

Banks, Charles E. *Winthrop Fleet of 1630.* New York: Houghton Mifflin, 1930.

Caffrey, Kate. *The Mayflower.* New York: Stein and Day, 1974.

Cressy, David. *Coming Over: Migration and Communication between England and New England in the Seventeenth Century.* New York: Cambridge University Press, 1987.

Cunnington, Phillis and Buck, Anne. *Children's Costume in England from the Fourteenth to the End of the Nineteenth Century.* New York: Barnes and Noble, 1965.

Demos, John. *A Little Commonwealth: Family Life in Plymouth Colony.* New York: Oxford University Press, 1970.

Earle, Alice M. *Child Life in Colonial Days.* New York: MacMillan, 1899.

Fischer, David Hackett. *Albion's Seed: Four British Folkways in America.* New York: Oxford University Press, 1989.

Hall, David D. *Worlds of Wonder, Days of Judgment: Popular Religious Belief in Early New England.* New York: Alfred A. Knopf, 1989.

Hunt, William. *The Puritan Moment: Coming of Revolution in an English County.* Cambridge: Harvard University Press, 1983.

Jebb, Miles, ed. *East Anglia: An Anthology.* London: Barrie & Jenkins, 1990.

Laurence, Anne. *Women in England: 1500–1760.* New York: St. Martin's Press, 1994.

Mather, Increase. *Remarkable Providences.* New York: Arno Press, 1977.

Nickerson, W. Sears. *Land Ho! 1620: A Seaman's Story of the Mayflower.* East Lansing, Mich: Michigan State University Press, 1997.

Patten, John. *English Towns 1500–1700.* London: Dawson Archon Books, 1978.

Steer, Francis, W. *Farm and Cottage Inventories of Mid-Essex 1635–1749.* London: Phillimore, 1969.

Willison, George. *The Pilgrim Reader: The Story of the Pilgrim as Told by Themselves & Their Contemporaries Friendly and Unfriendly.* Garden City, NY: Doubleday & Co. Inc., 1953.

PERIODICALS

Le Guin, Charles. "Sea Life in Seventeenth Century England," *American Neptune* 27 (1967): 111–34.

McElroy, John. "Seafaring in Seventeenth Century New England," *New England Quarterly* 8 (1935): 331–64.

Stein, Roger B. "Seascape and the American Imagination: The Puritan Seventeenth Century," *Early American Literature* 7 (1972): 17–37.

About the Author

Trained as a journalist, Laurie Lawlor worked for many years as a freelance writer and editor before devoting herself full-time to the creation of children's books. She enjoys many speaking engagements at schools and libraries, and her books have been nominated for many awards. She lives in Evanston, Illinois, with her husband, son, daughter, and two large Labrador retrievers. Her books include the *Addie Across the Prairie* series, the *Heartland* series, *How to Survive Third Grade*, *The Worm Club*, *Gold in the Hills*, and *Little Women* (a movie novelization). Her nonfiction work, *Shadow Catcher: The Life and Work of Edward S. Curtis*, won the Carl Sandburg Award for nonfiction (1995) and the Golden Kite Honor Book Award (1995).